Enderby's Dark Lady

novels

The Long Day Wanes:
    Time for a Tiger
    The Enemy in the Blanket
    Beds in the East
The Right to an Answer
The Doctor is Sick
The Worm and the Ring
Devil of a State
One Hand Clapping
A Clockwork Orange
The Wanting Seed
Honey for the Bears
Inside Mr Enderby
Nothing like the Sun: A Story
    of Shakespeare's Love-Life
The Eve of Saint Venus
A Vision of Battlements
Tremor of Intent
Enderby Outside
MF
Napoleon Symphony
The Clockwork Testament;
    or, Enderby's End
Beard's Roman Women
Abba Abba
Man of Nazareth
1985
Earthly Powers
The End of the World News

for children

A Long Trip to Teatime
The Land Where the
    Ice Cream Grows

verse

Moses

non-fiction

English Literature: A Survey
    for Students
They Wrote in English
Language Made Plain
Here Comes Everybody: An
    Introduction to James Joyce for
    the Ordinary Reader
The Novel Now: A Student's Guide
    to Contemporary Fiction
Urgent Copy: Literary Studies
Shakespeare
Joysprick: An Introduction to
    the Language of James Joyce
New York
Hemingway and His World
On Going to Bed
This Man and Music

translator

The New Aristocrats (with Llewela
    Burgess)
The Olive Trees of Justice (with
    Llewela Burgess)
The Man Who Robbed Poor Boxes
Cyrano de Bergerac
Oedipus the King

editor

The Grand Tour
Coaching Days of England
A Shorter Finnegans Wake

ANTHONY BURGESS

Enderby's Dark Lady

or No End to Enderby

Composed to placate kind readers of
The Clockwork Testament, or Enderby's End,
who objected to my casually killing
my hero

Hutchinson

London Melbourne Sydney Auckland Johannesburg

Hutchinson & Co. (Publishers) Ltd

An imprint of the Hutchinson Publishing Group

17-21 Conway Street, London W1P 6JD

Hutchinson Publishing Group (Australia) Pty Ltd
PO Box 496, 16-22 Church Street, Hawthorne, Melbourne,
Victoria 3122

Hutchinson Group (NZ) Ltd
32-34 View Road, PO Box 40-086, Glenfield, Auckland 10

Hutchinson Group (SA) (Pty) Ltd
PO Box 337, Bergvlei 2012, South Africa

First published 1984
Reprinted 1984
© Anthony Burgess 1984

Set in Linotron Plantin by Input Typesetting Ltd
London SW19 8DR

Printed and bound in Great Britain by Anchor Brendon Ltd
Tiptree, Essex

ISBN 0 09 156050 0

A Prefatory Note

Enderby first got into my head in early 1959, when I was a colonial civil servant working in the Sultanate of Brunei, North Borneo. One day, delirious with sandfly fever, I opened the door of the bathroom in my bungalow and was not altogether surprised to see a middle-aged man seated on the toilet writing what appeared to be poetry. The febrile vision lasted less than a second, but the impossible personage stayed with me and demanded the writing of a novel about him. I wrote half this novel in 1960, a year in which the medical authorities had condemned me to death with an inoperable cerebral tumour. It did not appear that there would be time to write the second part of the novel, so I published the first part as a whole book under the title of *Inside Mr Enderby*. To the chagrin of the doctors, who did not like their prognosis to be proved false, I lived and was able, in 1967, to write the second part of the novel, under the title of *Enderby Outside*. A few years later Enderby demanded that he be killed off in a novella entitled *The Clockwork Testament*. I duly murdered him with a heart attack. Now, in this new brief novel, he is alive again. It seems that fictional characters, though they sometimes may have to die, are curiously immune to death. Is Don Quixote dead or alive? Is Hamlet? Is Little Nell? Enderby's demand to be resurrected has come inconveniently, for I am engaged on a longish novel about Nero and St Paul.

A decent respect to people's notions of plausibility demands that I try to explain why Enderby, having died of a heart attack in New York about ten years ago, should be alive three years later in the state of Indiana. (And why Indiana, a part of the United States I do not know very well?) I think we have to look at it this way: all fictional events are hypotheses, and the condition of Enderby's going to live in New York would be that he should die there. If the hypothesis is unfulfilled, he does not have to die. Enderby was condemned to visit the United States, there to suffer, and there was a choice between his going to Manhattan to teach Creative Writing and his being employed to write the libretto for a ridiculous musical about Shakespeare in a fictitious theatre in Indianapolis. He took the second course, which involved his staying alive to risk a suicidal identification (himself with the Bard) but to come through unscathed. He will, of course, eventually die, but only because his creator will die. On the other hand, being a fictional character, he cannot die.

Enderby's name comes from two sources – the remote and uninhabitable Antarctic territory called Enderby Land, and a poem about a shipwreck by Jean Ingelow in which church bells clang out a tune called 'The Brides of Enderby'. His poems are, inevitably, written by myself, but only myself in disguise as Enderby. A reviewer in *Punch* said, of the first novel or half-novel, 'It would be helpful if Mr Burgess could indicate somewhere whether these poems are meant to be good or bad,' a fine instance of critical paralysis. T. S. Eliot liked at least three of the poems, but posterity is beginning to find his taste unsure, especially since he too, like Enderby, became the librettist for a Broadway musical. I have no opinion about either Enderby's poems or Enderby himself. I do not know whether I like or dislike him; I only know that, for me, he exists. I fear that he may probably go on existing.

A. B.
Lugano, November 1983

1 Will and Testament

When Ben Jonson was let out of jail he went straight to William Shakespeare's lodgings in Silver Street and said: 'Let us drink.'

'Ben,' Will cried. 'Your ears are untrimmed and your nose whole. The shearers were held off, then. I'm glad to see you well.'

'But thirsty. Let us go and drink.'

'We can drink here and shall. Malmsey? Sherrisack? Or shall I send out for ale? Ben Ben Ben, have a care. Next time the shearer may be the ultimate trimmer, the sconce-chopper as they call him.'

'I've a mind to drink in a tavern. Let us go.'

'As you will, this being a sort of great day for you. How was it in jail? Are Marston and Chapman there yet?'

'There still and like to stay. After all, the offending line was of their making. As for the jail – stink, maggots, rats, lepers, pocky chancres. But there was a man I will tell you of while we drink.'

'You swore to me the line was your line, the best line in the whole of *Westward Ho* as you would have it. How does it go now? "The Scotch –" It begins with "The Scotch –". '

'*Eastward Ho* is the title. You look as ever the wrong way. Back when the rest of us look forward. It is this: "The Scotch are good friends to England, but only when they are out of it." Well, indeed I wrote it, but it seemed politic to father it on the other two. Under oath, aye, but a poet could not live did he not perjure.' They went down the stairs and past the workshop of the tiremaker Mountjoy, Will's landlord. Mountjoy was scolding, in Frenchified English, the apprentice Belott.

'Immortal,' Will said. 'He can never say that I did not make him immortal. But no gratitude there.'

'How immortal?'

'I have him in *Harry Five* as the herald.'

'He taught you the dirty French for the same?'

'He put right the grammar. I knew the dirt already.' Out in Silver Street, which the sun had promoted to gold, they saw beggars, limbless soldiers, drunken sailors, whores, dead cats, ordinary decent citizens in stuff gowns, a kilted Highlander with a flask of usquebaugh in place of a sporran. A ballad singer with few teeth sang:

> 'For bonny sweet Robin was all my joy,
> And Robin came oft to my bed.
> But Robin did wrong, so to end his song
> The headsman did chop off his head.'

'An old one,' Ben said. 'And still I cannot hear it without a shudder.'

'It seems older than it is. A great deal has happened in the interim. Poor Robin.'

'That was your name for him? You called him Robin to his face?'

'He was Robin to my lord of Southampton, and my lord of Southampton was ever Harry to me. So it was always out-upon-titles. But, he was ever saying, when he was become King Robert the First of England there would be no familiarity then. Would it had been so, sometimes I think, though bloodless, bloodless.'

'Treason, man, careful.'

'What will you do, report me to Gobbo Cecil? "An't please you, good my lord, there is this low playmaker that doth say how the Essex rebellion should have succeeded." He'll say, "Aye aye, and maybe he's in the right of it." He's no love for slobbering Jamie with his bishops and buggery and drinking tobacco is an unco foul sin to the body, laddie, and doth inflame the lung, if thou lovest tobacco then lovest thou not thy king.'

Ben sighed. 'I know how it is. I say too many Scotchmen about and I am flung in jail. You could tell the king to his face that he's a – I say no more, you see that sour man in black there? Following us, is he? Nay, he turned off. You could skite in his majesty's mouth and he'd say, "Aye, I do dearly love a guid witty jest, laddie, will ye be raised to a Knicht o' the Garrrterrr?" Some men are born jail meat. Others – Here, round here. At the bottom of this lane. Go tipatoe, 'tis all slime underfoot. Careful, careful.'

'The Swan with Two Necks.' Will read the warped sign with a fastidious nose-wrinkle. 'This is not a tavern I mind ever to have visited before.'

'It is quiet,' Ben said, leading the way into noise, stench, striding over a vomit pool, between knots of swarthy men with daggers. 'We can talk in peace and quiet.' They sat on a settle before a rickety much-punished table whereon fat flies fed amply from greasy orts and a sauce-smear unwiped. A girl with warty bosom well on show showed black teeth and took an order for wine. 'Red wine,' Ben said. 'Of your best. Blood-red, red as the blood of our blessed Saviour.' Some villains turned to look with surly interest. A man with an eyepatch nodded as in friendly threat at Ben. 'Buenos dias, señor,' Ben said.

'For God's sake, Ben, what manner of place is this?'

'A good place, though something filthy. Good fellows all, though but rogues to look on. Now let me speak. A great change is come into my life.'

The wine arrived. Will poured. 'Change? You have fallen in love with some pocked tib of the Clink and think her to be a disguised angel?'

'Ah, no. By heaven, this is good wine, red, aye, red as the blood that is decanted daily on the blessed holy altars of the one true faith.'

'For Christ's sake, Ben.'

'Aye, for Christ's sake, you say truly. What I do I do for Christ's dear sake. Let me tell you, my dear friend, what befell. In this noisome stinking rathole behold the word of the Lord came to me.'

'Oh Jesus the word of the.'

'Aye, a good old priest of the true faith, aye, though earning his bread as a dancing-master, thrown into jail for debt, spake to me loving words and told where the truth doth lie. It was by way of being in the manner somewhat of a revelation.' Ben drank fiercely and then said: 'Good wine. *Enim calix sanguinis.* Drink a salute to my holy happiness.'

'Keep your voice well down, man,' Will said, his voice well down. 'See how they all listen.'

'They may listen and be glad. I have friends, have I not? Have I not friends here?' he called to the drinkers. '*Amigos?*' There was no response save for a man hawking, though all looked still.

'I am getting out of here,' Will said.

'Aye, ever the prudent. Well, there is another word for prudent and you know it well. A plague on all cowards. Why should I not speak aloud my joy in being restored to the one true holy bosom? Is not the Queen's self of the blessed company? I tell you, the day is at hand when we may take the holy body in sunlight before the eyes of all men, not skulking in a dark hole. Hallelujah.'

'You know the danger, fool,' Will said, sweating. 'There was an expectation of tolerance, but it is not fulfilled. The bishops will see it is not. Let us be out of here.'

'With this blessed red wine unfinished? With this blood of the grape crimson as the blood of.'

'I am going.' Will drained the sour stuff and turned down his cup with a clank.

'Well, well, very well, I have told my story. Now, thanks be to God, my true story doth begin.' Ben drank straight from the jug, beastlily, emerging spluttering. He wiped his mouth with the dirty back of his hand and nodded in a friendly manner at the company. 'Give you good day, all. And God's blessing be ever on your comings and goings and eke your staying where you are.'

'Come, idiot.'

They left. Ben said, 'Aye, aye, we will see how the spirit works. Is anyone following?'

'None. None yet. Do you wish someone to follow?'

'I say no more of it now, Ben Jonson his conversion. Except that you may speak of it to your friends and colleagues and all you will. I care not. I dare all for the lord Jesus. I owe him a death.'

'That is mine. I wrote that.'

'You did? It is all one. There is a tale they tell of you, do you know that?'

'What tale? Where?'

'Jack Marston told me. It is of Master Shakespeare dead and ascending to heaven's gate and demanding admittance. St Peter says: We have too many landlords here, we need poets to sweeten long eternity. Well, says Master Shakespeare, I am well known to be a poet. Prove it, says St Peter. I am of poor memory, says Master S, and can remember no line I wrote. Well then, says heaven's warder, extemporize somewhat. At that moment within the gates and all visible from the threshold little bow-legged Tom Kyd goes by, a poetic martyr, with his fingers cruelly broke by the late Queen's Commissioners. A bow-legged one, says the saint. Extemporize on him. Whereupon, firequick, Master S comes out with:

'How now, what manner of man is this
That beareth his balls in parenthesis?'

'Whereupon St Peter sighs and says: We have no room for landlords.'

'Not funny,' Will said. And then: 'So they talk of me as dead already, do they?'

'Not dead. Shall we say retired. Your sun setteth. Westward Ho is your cry.' Ben looked behind him to see two daggered ruffians following. He said in some small excitement: 'Leave me here. Take your leave, aye. I think there are two coming who will show me where I may hear mass Sundays and saint-days. The blessing of Mother Church on you, Will.'

'No, no, I want no such blessing.'

It was some week or so later that Ben Jonson sat at dinner with new friends, the room being an upper one in Eastcheap. There was Bob Catesby at the head of the table, very fierce and sober, and a swarthy one that had been in that low tavern that time they called Guy though his true name was Guido, somewhat drunk on Spanish wine, and there were Rob Winter, little big-eyed Bates, Kit Wright, Tom Winter brother of Rob, and also Frank Tresham who kept wetting a dry lip and looking shifty. Catesby said to Ben:

13

'You are wide open, Master Jonson. Your days are numbered.'

'By whom?' Ben said. 'If you mean that I blab of the brotherhood, by God you are mistaken.'

'You have not done that, no, you have been prudent enough there. If you had not been so, Guy here – a soldier, remember, who will cut off ten heads before his breakfast – Guy, I say, would have had you, by God. No, I mean imprudent in that you talk too much of the Godless King and the runagate Queen, who will show her bosom and legs to all and go to mass hiccuping with the drink. I mean treasonable talk. I believe you are destined for a martyr's crown.'

'No,' Ben said. 'I want not that. I will not force apart the jaws of heaven for my precocious entering. Heaven may open in its own good time without my prompting. There is wine for the drinking yet and wenches for the fondling. Nay, no martyrdom.'

'Speak out the scheme, Rob,' Catesby said to Tom Winter's brother. 'You are he that must hold it in his memory. You are our living parchment.'

'Well, then,' Rob Winter said, looking at Ben, 'it is this. It is to do with the new session of the parliament. All will be there – King, Queen, Prince Henry, nobles, judges, knights, esquires and all, all for the forging of new acts and laws to put down the true faith. They will be blown up.'

'They will be –?' Ben asked carefully.

'Blown up. We are to place twenty barrels of gunpowder in the cellar beneath with faggots on top. Set but flame to the faggots and there will be a greater blowing up than has ever before been seen in the long tale of tyranny and human suppression.'

'Blown up,' Catesby said after a pause, as to make sure Ben properly understood.

'The Queen,' Ben said, 'is of the true faith. Is it right she too should be blown up?'

'You are always ready to talk of her Godlessness,' Catesby said. 'Well, she will be punished. Alternatively, she will be a martyr. Destiny puts forth a choice.'

'However you gloss it,' Ben said, 'she will be blown up.'

'Everybody will be blown up,' Tom Winter said, pausing in

the picking of his teeth. They had eaten of a roast ham, each mouthful full of teeth-hugging fibres. 'Everybody.'

'And then there will be a new era of love for the true faith?' Ben asked.

'We will think of that after the blowing up,' Catesby said. 'Certainly there will be a many problems, but sufficient to the day as the Gospel saith. First the blowing up.'

'And the choice of the one to whom shall be given the glory of setting flame to the faggots for the blowing up,' Kit Wright said. They all now looked at Ben.

'He too will be blown up?' Ben asked.

'There is every likelihood that he will be blown up,' Catesby said. 'But he will at once be endued with a crown of martyrdom. You, Master Jonson, are wide open.' They all continued to look at Ben. Ben said:

'How first are you to convey the barrels to the cellar?'

'It is a wine cellar,' Rob Winter said. 'The barrels will be brought on a vintner's dray. What have you there, the guards will ask. Wine, will come the answer. Wine, as hath been ordered. It is all very simple.'

'And the faggots?'

'The faggots will be in another barrel, dry and ready for the laying on. And he that is to do the brave deed will go as a guard in a borrowed livery. Bearing a torch.'

'In broad daylight?' Ben asked.

'He will say he has orders to search the cellar for possible treasonous men lurking. It is all very simple.'

Francis Tresham now spoke. 'I am against it,' he said. 'It is a plot of some cruelty. Also of some injustice. The Queen, true, is a foreigner and doth not matter. But there are enow good Catholic Englishmen in hiding among those of the parliament. We are blowing up our own.'

'Martyrs' crowns,' Ben said. 'Think not of it.'

'You will do the deed?' Catesby said, leaning closer to Ben and, indeed, discharging a blast of hammy garlic onto him.

'I will think on it,' Ben said. 'Your reasons are of a fairly persuadent order. I will go home now and start to think on it.'

'Guy here will go home with you,' Catesby said, 'and help you think on it.'

'No, he will not,' Ben said. 'I want none breathing on me

15

while I think. I go into this in full *libero arbitrio*. I cannot be made to do it.'

'That is true,' Catesby said. 'Except by the promptings of your own destiny, Master Jonson. I see the martyr's crown hovering above you.' He looked somewhat fiercely at Tresham. 'Frank,' he said, 'you waver. It is strange you waver when you were loudest once in saying perdition to the betrayer of the faith of his own royal mother. There are measures may be taken to discourage waverers.' He looked at dark Guido and then back at pale Tresham.

'I am no waverer. I ask only that we right our souls on this matter of the killing of Catholics along with Protestants. It is a matter of theology I would ask that we concern ourselves withal.'

'Theology,' little Bates now said. 'There is enow of theology at the Godless court, holy Jamie and his atheistical bishops. Out on theology. Let us have the true faith back and God's enemies blown up. I drink to you,' he said, 'Master Jonson,' and drank.

'I too drink to me,' Ben said, and drank likewise. He wiped his loose lips and wrung his beard and said, looking at the company severally, 'Now I go home. To pray. For blessing and eke for guidance.'

'Guido will go with you for guidance through the perilous streets,' Catesby said.

'I go alone. I am in no peril.'

'Guy will be your guide.'

Ben, with Guido Fawkes at his flank, was some way advanced through the warren of stinks and drunkenness and stinking drunken bravoes that led to his lodgings when, to keep up his courage, he began to sing:

> 'Here will we sit upon the rocks
> And see the shepherds feed their flocks
> By shallow rivers to whose falls
> Melodious birds sing madrigals.'

At the song Fawkes clicked his fingers and said:
   'Spy.'
   'I cry your mercy, what was that?'

'Spy, I said. I think you to be a manner of spy.'

Ben ceased walking or rolling and looked at him fair and straight beneath the moon. 'You are drunk, man. You know not what you say.'

'Spy. I asked myself long who it was you put me in mind of, and he too was a poet and spy. He cried his sodomitical atheism to the streets, and none did him harm. I conclude he was under protection. His name was Kit Marlowe. That was a song of his you were singing but now. Spy.'

'Marlowe,' Ben said soberly. 'He was all our fathers, though he was slain young, God help him. You flatter me more than you know. But I am no spy.' They heard as it were antiphonal singing, though more drunk than sober, approach.

'Sit we amid the ewes and tegs
Where pastors custodise their gregs
And cantant avians do vie
With fluminous sonority.'

'O Jesus,' Ben prayed. 'Jack Marston.'

It was Marston, true, drunk, true, but able to see, mainly from the bulk, who stood in his path. 'Jonson, cheat, rogue, liar, ingrate, thief too. I am out now, see, and have learned all. Graaagh.' The sound was of blood rising in the throat.

'You speak too plain to be true Marston. Where be your inkhorn nonsensicalities? Thief, you say. No man says thief to Jonson. Any more,' he added to Fawkes, 'than he says spy.'

'Thief I say again. You said that you would pay me when Henslowe paid you, that Henslowe had not paid you, therefore you could not pay me. But Henslowe has paid you, has, thief. I was with him this night, I saw his account book. Draw, thief.' He drew himself, though staggering.

'If it is but six shilling and threepence you want, let us have no talk of drawing. Come to my lodgings and you shall have a little on account. I will not have that *thief*, Jack. I am a man of probity and of religion.'

'Of that we hear too,' Marston cried. 'The lactifluous nipples of the Christine genetrix and the viniform sanguinity of the eucharistic abomination. Draw.'

'Very well.' Ben sighed and unsheathed his short dagger. 'I

have killed, Jack,' he said, 'and my adversary was sober. I killed Gab Spencer, remember, and he too said *thief*.' Ben now saw the reflection of flames in a bottle-paned window. Torches lurching round the corner of Cow Lane. Four men with swords and cudgels, the watch. With relief he lunged towards Marston. Lunging, he saw Fawkes flee. Wanted no trouble, right too, right for his filthy cause. Marston thrust, tottered, fell. Ben sheathed his dagger and leapt onto Marston's back, took his ears like ewer handles and began to crack his nose into the dirt of the cobbles. Then the watch was on him.

It was four of the morning when Will received the message to go at once to the Marshalsea. A boy hammered at the door below and Will went to his window, Mountjoy in his nightshirt also appearing, a minute later, at his.

'Mester Shakepaw?'

'Approximately. What, boy?'

'Mester Jonson in the jail do want ye naow vis minik.'

'He wants money?'

'I fink not sao. E gyve me manny, a ole groat, see ere.'

'Go away, garsoon,' Mountjoy cried harshly, 'discommoding the voisinage so. We desire no parlying of prisons in this quartier. It is a quartier respectable.'

'I'll come,' Will sighed. 'I'll come now.'

Few were sleeping in the Marshalsea. There was a kind of growling merriness, with drink, cursing, fumbling at plackets, gaming, a richer though darker version of the dayworld of the free. There was even a one-eyed man selling hot possets. Will listened, sipping, to Ben's story. 'The names,' Ben said, 'take down the names.'

'I can remember well enough of the names.'

'You cannot. You are poor at remembering. You cannot remember even your own lines. Take your tablet, take down the names. And then to Cecil.'

'Now?'

'Now, yes. Easy enough for you. You're a groom of the bedchamber, a sort of royal officer.'

'This is no jape?'

'This is by no manner of means a jape, God help us. Go. I am, thank God, safe enough here. Cecil will understand all that, why I wish to be shut away. I am safe enough here till he has them.'

'I will write them down, then.'

'Do, quick. Then go.'

'So,' Will said. 'Kit is truly your master. Though look where his spying got him. A reckoning in a little room. Keep off it, Ben. Playwork is duller and pays less well. But it is safer.'

'Go now. He will be up. He does a day's work before breakfast.'

Will sat, in groom's livery, too long in the anteroom. He had spoken of his business to secretaries of progressively ascending status, and none would come alive to the urgency of it. One had even said: 'If you would speak of plots for new plays, then must you go to the Lord Chamberlain. Here be grave matters in hand.'

'You will be at no graver work than the scotching of this that I tell you of.' Weary, three hours gone by, Will took to sketching of a drinking song he had been asked for by Beaumont, something for a comedy to be called *Have at You Now Pretty Rogue* or some such nonsense:

> Red wine it is the soldier's blood
> And if it be both old and good
> So take a rouse
> And let's carouse
> And

Strange, he had been infected by Ben's feigned unreformed eucharisticism. No, it was tother way around. Blood turned to wine, not wine to. His head was spinning with lack of sleep, he needed much sleep these days, past his best, looking westward. He began to calculate his fortune in real estate, but that led him to things needful to be done in Stratford. The load of stone still encumbering the grounds of New Place and neither paid for yet by the Council nor taken away. His brother Gilbert had written of some odd useful acres he might – He was shaken to here and now by the top secretary, who said:

'You are to come in. And quickly, rouse. My lord speaks of urgency.'

'He was not very urgent in speaking of it.'

'Come your ways.'

Robert Cecil, Earl of Salisbury, big-headed and dwarf-bodied, stood with his hunchback turned to the great seacoal fire. Papers, papers everywhere. He said:

'I am glad, albeit it be brief, to make acquaintance of the man. The plays I know. Your *Amblet* was fine comedy. What is this story?'

Will told him. 'And Master Jonson fears for his life now. He deserves, if I may say this, my lord, very well of you.'

Cecil picked up a letter from his desk. 'This has but now come to me. You know of a certain Francis Tresham Esquire?'

'His name is, I think, on the list I gave.'

'He has a brother-in-law, Lord Monteagle. Lord Monteagle has sent me a letter from this Tresham, and it saith nought but this: "They shall receive a terrible blow this parliament, and yet they shall not see who hurts them. The danger is past as soon as you have burnt this letter." As you see, it was not burnt, nor will it be. I am conveying it at once to His Majesty. So what you bring from Master Jonson conjoined with this does but confirm what the King will say he knew all along, that he hath enemies.' Cecil smiled very thinly. 'Moreover, it would seem that his dreams are often charged with what may be termed a *memoria familiaris*. Blowing up comes much into them. His father, the Lord Darnley, was, as you will know, blown skyhigh at Kirk-o-Fields in Scotland while his royal mother was dancing at some rout or other. So, I thank you for this your loyal work – '

'A tragedy, good my lord.'

'It might well have been so.'

'No, no, my play, which some call *Hamlet*.'

'Was it so? I remember laughing. Now I will remember the intention was tragic. And remember too to have Master Jonson out of the jail where he languisheth as soon as the conspirators be apprehended.' Cecil gave his hand, very crusty with rings, to Will. Will was not sure whether he was meant to kiss it. But he shook it sturdily and left.

When Ben Jonson was let out of jail he went straight to William Shakespeare's lodgings in Silver Street and said:

'Let us drink.'

'Ben,' Will said, 'if you mean we are to go again to this low papist tavern full of vomit – '

'Nay, show sense, man, that was but show. That was part of the part I played and played well. I am as good a son of the English Church as any that was fried under Bloody Mary, and I will prove it Sunday by drinking the whole chalice off before all the world. I say let us drink. I say also let us eat, it being near noon. I have good King's gold here.' He made jangle the little purse at his waist or no-waist. Clink clank. 'We will eat roach pie and flawns at the Mermaid.'

Ben told it all over the fishbones and pasty fragments. 'Of course,' he said, 'the King will have it that he foreknew all. Let them, says he, get in theirrr Godless butts of gunpowderrr and I myself, laddies, will marrrch thither with guarrrd and witness to prrrove it was no tale. So he did, and so he says that he has singlehanded saved the rrrealm. Will you come to the hanging?'

'I will not.'

'Squeamish as ever. Twelve men swinging aloft in the sun and enow guts and blood and hearts ripped out to feed the King's kennels a whole day. There is a little book to come,' he coughed modestly.

'I thought you were waiting to print all your plays, such as they be, in one great book called Ben Jonson's *Works*, mad notion. Or is it epigrams and corky expatiations all in Greco-Latin?'

'I will let pass your pleasantries. This little book will have no name of author below the title, though all shall know from the mastery whose it is. The title is to be *A Discourse of the Manner of the Discovery of the Late Intended Treason*.'

'That is too long.'

'Have a care, man. It is the King's own. And it is to be spread abroad that the King's self had the writing of it but was too royally modest to set his name thereto. It is a terrible false world.'

Will now quoted from something he was writing. 'We have seen the best of our time. Machinations, hollowness, treachery, and all ruinous disorders follow us disquietly to our graves.'

'You sound as though you cite somewhat from some new kennel of misery you are hammering together unhandily.'

'A tragedy, aye. About a king that insists on divine right and knee-killing deference and fulsome fawning and will not have the plain truth. He is cast out into the cold and goes mad and dies.'

'A care, Will, a care.'

'It is for the court.'

'O Jesus, O blood of Christ not really present on the altar. You will be hanged and quartered like any Guy Fawkes.'

'I care not. We have seen the best of our time.'

When Christmas came to court, Lear, done by Dick Burbage, ranted and tore his beard, and Queen Anne slept or woke and pouted at what seemed most unseasonable for Yule, a time of drunken showing of one's legs in some pretty wanton masque, while James drank steadily and chewed kickshawses offered by a succession of lords on bended knee. After the play he ranted. The Grooms of the Royal Bedchamber were there, in livery after their acting, yawning, Will among them, hound-weary, half-listening.

'Therrre ye see, my lorrrds and ladies and guid laddies a', what befalleth a king that trusts too much in human naturrre. It is the trrragedy of ane that insisteth not enough on his divine rrricht. He lets gang the rrrule o's rrrealm tae ithers. Weel, thank God though I hae drrrunken sons I hae nae ambitious dochters of yon stamp. Aye aye aye.' Then he suddenly shouted: 'Kingship, kingship, kingship,' so that many of the drowsy started full awake. 'I was but rrreading in the Geneva Bible this day, aye, and find therrre mickle to offend, aye. Much flouting I find of the divinity of kingship in the saucy marrrgins therrreof. Aye, I was in the rrricht of it, the divine rrricht I may say, to hae thrrrown oot of the rrrealm a buik nae matterrr hoo holy that hath been defiled by the pens of Godless rrrepublicans, aye. It is verrry parrrtial in its notes and glosses, verrry untrrrue, seditious, and savourrring tae much of dangerrrous and traitorrrous conceits. When, my lorrrd arrrchbishop, shall we see our ither, our new, our Godly?'

'They are hard at work, your grace,' said the Archbishop of Canterbury, huge archiepiscopal rings of weariness under his eyes. 'All fifty-four translators, all six companies. Andrewes and Harding and Lively report well of the progress of the holy work and say but four years more will see it sail gloriously all pennants flying into port.'

'So Harrrding looks lively and Lively labourrrs harrrd, eh, eh?' There was loud and immediate laughter that went on long while the King beamed around and said: 'Aye aye aye.'

Will could see that his majesty was looking in vain for a pun that should bring Lancelot Andrewes, head of the Westminster translating groups, into his fancy. Without premeditation Will came out, in a firm all too audible actor's voice, with:

> 'Each Bible scholar, so the ungodly say,
> Works *lively hard Eng*lishing for no pay
> The royal Bible, aye, *and rewes* the day
> When such an unholy labour came his way.'

There was a terrible silence into which the King waded rather than leapt. He said:

'And wha micht ye be, laddie? Wait noo, I ken, I ken, ye are he that wrrrit the play of this nicht, are ye not?'

'Aye, William Shakespearrre, yourrr majesty,' Will said, hearing with horror an effortless parody of the royal accent.

'Ye maun wrrrite it doon, yon saucy blasphemous irrreverrrent and impairrrtinent lump o' clairrrty doggerrrel, that all may see, laddie.'

'I have forgot it already, your royal majesty,' Will said, hearing in horror the faint traces of the sobbing Danish intonations of the Queen.

'Aye.' It was clear that James did not know well what to do. Will had often met this situation when being unpremeditatedly pert to the great. He now willed the King out of his problem. *Be sick, great greatness.* 'Aye, ye and yourrr saucy rrrhymes.' He looked green and began to heave. It was, indeed, the usual end of a court soirée. Some writer of music for the virginals, Tomkins or somebody, had spoken of producing a tiny sequence consisting of the King's Rouse, the King's Vomiting, the King's Rest. 'I maun gang,' the King said, very green. 'I mind ye, laddie, I'll mind yourrr sauciness.' Then, on the arms of two simpering earls, he was led away to the Harington water closet, invention of the late Queen's godson, Britain's contribution to the civilization of Europe.

'By Christ,' Burbage said, 'you get away with murder.'

'What Ben Jonson says. Thank God our revels now are ended, aye.'

When, much much time later, Ben Jonson was let out of jail he went straight to William Shakespeare's lodgings in Silver Street and said:

'Let us drink.'

'Ben,' Will cried. 'Your ears are untrimmed and your nose whole. I'm glad to see you well.'

'But thirsty.'

'Drink water then. It seems to me that less and less of wine makes in you more and more of oppugnancy. If this drunken watch-beating continues it will be a matter of one day's holiday between longer and longer lingerings in the Clink.'

'The Marshalsea. Listen. It was a strange time. I worked on the Bible.'

'What?' They went down the stairs, past Mountjoy scolding his daughter Marie for loving the apprentice Belott, into the street, demoted to lead by the dull day. There were more drunk about than usual, belike because of the dull day. 'The Bible, this I know, has already been worked on, nay worked out. They are at the great final stage of the galleys. And it is Harding and Lively and Andrewes, not you, that had the making of it. You are a man of some small reasonable talent, Ben, but you are no man of God. It is work for men of God that gratuitously or necessarily know Greek and Latin and Hebrew.'

'I know all those tongues,' Ben said. 'I can Hebrew you as well as any clipped rabbi. It is, indeed, the work that comes before the final launching that has made lively my days in the stinking rathole of the Marshalsea. For, since I am a poet, they brought to me the poesy of the Bible. Meaning Job and the Psalms and the like. You are a poet, they said. Tickle our sober accuracy into poetic life. So I dip quill in horn and correct the galleys to a diviner beauty.'

'Who brought the galleys and said all this to you?' Will said with some jealousy.

'Some man of the Westminster company – Bodkin or Pipkin or some such name. No whit abashed at the prospect of seeing God's work buffed and polished in a foul and pestilential prison.

24

The apostles, he said, were in prison before being variously crucified.'

'That will not be your fate. Whatever your fate is, it will not be that. That is the fate of the godly.' And then, before they entered the Dog Tavern, 'Is it you only of all our secular versifiers that are bidden trim the sails of the galleys?'

'Oh, there is Chapman, also Jack Donne – not properly secular, there is talk of his taking holy orders this year. Marston's name was mentioned but I was quick there. If, I said, you want a Bible that beginneth with *In the initialities of the mondial entities the Omnicompetent fabricated the celestial and terrene quiddities*, then have Jack Marston by all means. There were others mentioned, smaller men.'

'Was I,' Will asked, 'mentioned?'

They sat down not far from Beaumont and Fletcher with their one doxy who, being born under the sign of Libra, was fain to bestow kisses and clips equally on both. When the jug of canary came Ben was able to have his laugh out.

'Why do you laugh? What is risible in me or others or elsewhere?'

'There were special orders that you should not be brought in. No Latin or Greek nor Hebrew – that was brushed aside as of small moment. But the King has a long memory and himself said that he would not hae that quick laddie that was perrrt with his imperrrtinencies.'

'How do you know this?'

'There is some foolish rhyme fathered on you about the King sticking his lively harding andrew up the translators to make them come quicker and threatening to cut off their old and new testicles if they did not. It could not be you, it is too corky and bad even for you. But I will be kind. You shall not be out in the cold like the foolish virgins. I, Ben-oni, the Benjamin that Jacobus loveth, though he cannot keep me out of jail, I am ready to deliver sundry psalms into your palms.'

'Is there money in it?'

'Honour, glory, perhaps an eternal crown.'

'I am done with all writing,' Will said, 'even for money. I grow old, I grow old. I am forty-six this year. I will retire to Stratford and hunt hares and foxes.'

'You would rather be hunted with them. And you have said

this too often before of being done with writing. You will go and stay a week and then be back here thirsting to write some new nonsense. I know you.'

'You *poets*,' Will said, 'may keep your Bible. You may stuff your old and new testes up your apocrypha.'

'There speaketh sour envy. Well, we will keep it and be glad. For the day may come, some thousand years hence, when even the *Works* of Ben Jonson will be read little, but the bright eyes of Ben Jonson will flash out here and there in a breathtaking felicity of phrase from the green Eden of God's own book that may never die.'

'You may stick your holofernes up your methuselah.'

'Master Shakespeare,' said Frank Beaumont timidly, 'there is a matter we would talk of, to wit a collaboration betwixt you and us here.'

'She hath enough to do fumbling two let alone three.'

'I mean with Jack here and myself. A comedy called *Out on You Mistress Minx* which must be ready for rehearsing some two days from now and not yet started though the money taken. You are quick, sir, as is known. A night of work with Jack and me as amanuenses and it can be done. We can pay a shilling. It is safe here in a little bag in Kitty here her bosom.'

'I have done with writing,' Will said proudly. 'I go to tend my country estates. All you *poets* may stick your zimris up your cozbis.'

'Well bethought and *à propos* and *a proposito*. We were held up in our playwork by the need to work on the Song of Songs that is Solomon's for Dekker that hath an ague. Kitty here gave us a good phrase. Love, she said, is better than wine. Is not that'a good phrase?'

'She carries two fair-sized flagons on her, I see. If by love she means comfort more than intoxication, then she is not right.'

'*Comfort me with flagons*,' Beaumont said to Fletcher. '*Flagons* is better than *apples*. Make a note.'

'You may all,' Will said, getting up, 'comfort your deuteronomies with your right index leviticus. I go now.'

'It is jealousy,' Ben said when he had gone. 'He has no part in the holy work.'

Will rode to Stratford nevertheless with three or four psalms in galley proof in his saddlebag, a gift from Ben Jonson. He was to see what he could do with them; to Ben they seemed not to offer matter for further poeticization. But for Will there would be much non-writing work in Stratford, save for the engrossing of signatures. The hundred and twenty acres bought from the Coombes which Gilbert was managing ill: these must be worked well. Gardeners needed for gardens and orchards. The tithes in Old Stratford and Welcombe and Bishopston. He, Will, was now a lay rector, a front-pew gentleman. Thomas Greene, the town clerk, together with his bitch of a wife and the two beefy squallers named Grayston and Hamnet, Gray and Ham, should be out of New Place by now, the lease up on Lady Day, 1610, this year. Forty-six years of age. Four and six make ten. One of the psalms in his saddlebag was number 46.

New Place, when he got there, was bright as a rubbed angel, Anne his wife and Judith his daughter yet unmarried having nought much to do save buff and sweep and pick up hairs from the floor. The mulberry tree was doing well. Anne was fifty-four now and looked it. Ben was right: his home was a place for dreaming of going back to; he would be back in London before the month was up, nothing more certain. On his second day home a murmuration of blacksuited Puritans infested his living room. Anne gave them ale and seedcake. They had a session of disnoding a knotty dull point of scripture, something to do with Elijah or some other hairy unwiped prophet. When they came out of the living room to find Will poking for wood-worm at a timber in the hall, they sourly nodded at him as if to begrudge his being in his own house. The following day they came again for a prayer meeting. He spoke mildly to Anne about this black or Brownist intrusion.

'While I am here,' he said, 'I will not have it. Tell them that, tell them I will not have it.'

'They are godly,' she said, 'and a blessing on the house.'

'I can do without their blessing. Besides, their aliger faces show no warmth of blessing.'

'They know what you are.'

'I am a gentleman with an escutcheon. I am, moreover, one of the King's servants. I am, I do not deny, also a player and a playmaker, but that was the step to being a gentleman. Will they begrudge me my ambition?'

'Plays are ungodly, as is known. They will have no plays in this town. Nor will it avail you aught to flaunt your king's livery in their faces. They know that kings are mortal men and subject to the will of the Lord.'

'Genevan saints, are they? Holy republicans? What do they say of Gunpowder Plot?'

'They said that it showed at least a king might be punished for his sins by an action of the people, though to put down the Scarlet Woman of Rome is no sin and the voice of a papist is no part of the voice of the people.'

'God help us, Christ give us all patience.'

'You blaspheme, you see, you are in need of the power of prayer.'

'I am in need of nothing, woman, save a quiet life after a feverish one. I would have some seedcake with my ale.'

'There is no crumb left and there has been no time for baking.'

'If you must give up your hussif's duties in the name of dubious godliness, at least there is an idle daughter who could set to and bake.'

'Judith hath a green melancholy on her. It is a sad life for the girl. None asks for her hand.'

'Ah, they cannot stomach to have a player as a father-in-law. Well, at least Jack Hall takes me as I am. Jack is a poor physician but a good son-in-law and husband and father. Susannah, thank God, has done well.'

Susannah came next afternoon, with her husband Dr Hall and little two-year-old Elizabeth. Will played happily with the child and sang, in a cracked baritone, 'Where the Bee Sucks'. Anne said with suspicion:

'Is that from a play?'

'Not yet. The play that it is to be in is not yet writ, but it will be, fear not.'

'I fear not anything,' Anne said, 'save the Lord's displeasure.' She called to Judith to bring in ale and seedcake. Seeing married Susannah and the child now drowsy on her lap, Judith let out a howl of frustration and left. Anne said:

'It is the father's office to seek a husband for a daughter. Judith is ripe and over-ripe.'

'So ripeness is not after all all,' Will sighed. 'I will go seek in the taverns and hedgerows, crying *Who will wed a player's brat?*' He turned to Jack Hall, whose lips were pursed, and said, 'Will you come stroll a little in the garden?'

Jack said, after a strolling silence, 'Your book has been read here, you may know that.'

'What book?'

'The book that is called *Sonnets*.'

'But God, man, that is old stuff, it came out all of a year ago, and I have disclaimed the book, I did not publish it, it is pirate work. What do they say that read it, not that I care, does it confirm them in their conviction of Black Will Shakebag's damnation?'

'It is a book of things that a man might do in London,' Jack Hall said gloomily. 'It is pity that Dick Field brought home a copy.'

'Ah, poor corrupted Stratford. So you too join the headwaggers?'

'There is such a thing as propriety. Dick Field has been long a London man like yourself, father-in-law, but he has ever shown propriety. He hath printed foul stuff enow in his trade of printing, but he hath not the filthy ink of printed scandal sticking to him. You will, I trust, forgive the observation of one who is, besides your daughter's husband, a professional man and also your physical adviser.'

'Dick Field is a man tied to a cold craft, not one like me who has had to make himself a motley to the view and unload his naked soul to the world.' Then he said, 'What has being my physical adviser to do with the book that is called *Sonnets*?'

'I have wondered at times about your cough and your premature baldness. Now I read records of licentiousness in that book.'

'You mean,' groaned Will, then gasped, then growled, then cried aloud, 'I have the French pox, the disease of that pretty shepherd Syphilis of Fracastorius of Verona his poem? Oh, this drinks deep, this drinks the cup and all. And what thinks your sainted mother-in-law?'

'She knows nought of it. The book has been kept from her

and from her friends the brethren. The bridge of the nose,' he said, squinting, 'seems soft in the cartilage. That is an infallible sign. Do keep your voice low. It will crack if you shout out so and not easily be mended.'

Will howled like a hound and strode into the house to his study, passing his womenfolk on the way. He growled at them, even at gooing little Elizabeth. In his study he took from a drawer the galleys of the psalms that Ben had given him. He took them, waving in the draught of his passage, to shake like little banners at his family, crying, 'These, you see these? The King's new Bible that is not to appear until next year, given to me in part, along with my brethren the other poets of London, that the language be strengthened and enriched. You think me godless and a libertine but it is to me, me, me, not the black crows of Puritans that daily infest this house and shall not infest it more that the task of improving the word of the Lord is given. You see,' he said to Anne, 'you see, see?'

'A new Bible,' she said. 'It is all too like what one may expect of unreligious London, where the holy Geneva Bible is not good enough for them. That it is the King's Bible renders it no whit more holy. Nay, less from what we hear. Even kings are subject to the law.'

'The King,' Will cried, 'is my master and bathed in the chrism of the Lord God. Generous and good and holy.' Then he stopped, seeing he had gone too far. 'The King hath his faults,' he now said. Yes, indeed: ingratitude to Ben and himself: pederasty; immoderate appetite; cowardice, but half the man the old Queen had been. 'But still,' he said, and then: 'All men have their faults, myself included. But I deserve better of the world and of this little world, and, by God, I will have my eternal reward.'

'That,' said Anne, 'is the foul sin of presumption.' Jack Hall was now back with them, listening to his father-in-law rave, grow quiet, rave again: infallible symptoms.

'My name I mean, my name. My son, poor little Hamnet, dead. And the name Shakespeare dishonoured in its own town and soon to die out along with the poor parchments that put innocent words in the mouths of players.' Jack Hall shook his head slightly: self-pity too perhaps a symptom. 'Wait,' Will cried. 'Do not leave. I, your king, lord of this disaffected small commonweal, do order you to wait. Wait.' And he sailed back to the study, galley pennants flying, and took the forty-sixth psalm out of the bundle. He sat to it, calling 'Wait wait' as he dipped quill in ink and counted. Forty-six words from the beginning, then. It would do, the change improved not marred. He crossed out the word and put another large in the margin. He then, ignoring the cry or cadence *Selah* at the bottom, counted forty-six words from the end, felt awe at the miracle that this forty-sixth word too could be changed for the better, or certainly not for the worse, by the neat mark of deletion and the new word writ clear and large in the margin. 'Wait,' he cried. Then he was there to show them.

Anne's jaw dropped as in death. Susannah, whose sight was dim, squinnied at the thing he had done. Jack Hall said, 'This is also a – ,' and then kept his peace.

'You see, you see? To do this I have the right. I am not without right, do you see? Now another thing. On Sunday I will read this out in the church, aye, in Trinity Church during matins will I, and eke at evensong if I am minded to do it. For I am a lay rector. Not without right. And I have a voice that will fill the church to the rafters, not the piping nose-song of your scrawny unlay rector, do you hear me? *Non sanz droict*, which is the Shakespeare motto, and the name too shall prevail as long as the word of the Lord. Now, mistress,' he said to Anne, 'I would have supper served, and quickly.' Then he strode out to stand beneath his mulberry tree, granting her no time to rail.

On Sunday morning he stood, every inch a Christian gentleman in his neat London finery, on the altar steps of Trinity Church. Family, neighbours, the scowling brethren, shopkeepers, nosepicking children filled the pews. His voice, the voice of an actor, rose clear and strong:

'This Sunday you are to hear not the Lesson appointed for the day but the word of the Lord God in a form you do not know. Next year you will know it, for it is His Majesty King James's new Bible. But now you have this for the first time on any stage, I would say any altar. The word of the Lord. The forty-sixth psalm of King David.' He read from the galley expressively, an actor, clear, loud, without strain, so that all attended as they were in a playhouse and not in the house of God:

'God is our refuge and strength: a very present helpe in trouble. Therefore will not we feare, though the earth be removed: and though the mountaines be carried into the midst of the sea. Though the waters thereof roare and be troubled, though the mountaines ~~tremble~~ with the swelling thereof. Selah.

There is a river, the streames whereof shall make glad the citie of God: the holy place of the Tabernacles of the most High. God is in the midst of her: she shal not be mooved; God shall helpe her, and that right early.

The heathen raged, the kingdomes were mooved: he uttered his voyce, the earth melted. The Lord of hosts is with us; the God of Jacob is our refuge. Selah.

Come, behold the workes of the Lord, what desolations hee hath made in the earth. He maketh warres to cease unto the end of the earth: hee breaketh the bow, and

SPEARE/

cutteth the ~~sword~~ in sunder, he burneth the chariot in the fire.

Be stil, and know that I am God: I will bee exalted among the heathen, I will be exalted in the earth. The Lord of hosts is with us; the God of Jacob is our refuge. Selah.'

He ceased, looked fearlessly on them all, then stepped down, with an actor's grace, to return to his pew. One man at the back, forgetting where he was, began to applaud but was quickly hushed. Before Will arrived at his seat, Judith said to her mother:

'I wonder that God has not struck him down.'

'Wait,' Anne said grimly. 'The Lord does things in his own good time. Fear not, the Lord will repay.' Will sat down next to her. Then, having looked on her and Judith and Susannah and Jack Hall and Mrs Hart his sister with a peculiar lingering hardness, he knelt and prayed. He prayed long and with evident sincerity, so that his wife grew tight-mouthed with suspicion. Then he got up, looking much refreshed, sat down and waited till the dull long sermon was finished. Then he said very clearly to Anne and, indeed, to any on the pew that would hear:

'I am minded to turn papist.'

'God forgive you. Keep your voice down. This is not place nor time for atheistical japes.'

32

'I will turn papist.' He tasted the term gently then gently spat it out: *tpt*. 'I will not say that. It is a word of contempt. More, it puts overmuch emphasis on the Pope of Rome. It is the faith that matters.'

'Be quiet,' she said in quiet fury. The service was continuing, and eyes were on Will, ears striving to pick up his words.

'Catholic,' he said. Then he said no more. She remained tight-lipped. He did not speak of the matter again in the two days more he remained in Stratford.

When Ben Jonson was let out of jail he went straight to William Shakespeare's lodgings in Silver Street. Before he could say aught of going out to drink, Will said:

'I have writ this new play. It is called *November the Fifth*, but Burbage will doubtless change the title as he always does. It is based on Gunpowder Plot.'

Ben sat down carefully on a delicate French chair. 'It is based on – '

'Gunpowder Plot. There is a king that is a fool and an ingrate. He believes that God exists but to confirm the holiness of his kingship. Conspirators led by a poet seek to destroy him for his blasphemy.'

'A *poet*?'

'I had you much in my mind there. Not a very good poet and most apt for meddling in state matters. His name is Vitellius. Here is one of his speeches. Listen.'

'No,' Ben said. 'Let me read instead.' He looked at the fair copy that was also the first draft and read to himself:

> Conserve agst ye putrifyinge feende
> The fathe yt fedde oure fathers, quite put doune
> His incarnacioun in thes worst of tymes,
> Casting hys hedde discoronate to ye dogges.

Then he said: 'They will not let you. This will be construed as present treason.'

'I am sick of it all,' Will said. 'The black bastards of Puritans in Stratford that will have nothing but grimness, and a church that is the lapdog of a slobbering king and no king. My father died quietly in the old faith, I will die more noisily in it.'

'Have you spoke of this yet to any?'

'To my lord Cecil, aye, and he said he needed no more spies aping to be papists to dig out popish plots. I have said it to many, but none will take it that I mean what I say. It is part of the peril of being a player, that all one says is thought to be but acting.'

Ben said, 'The great work is now in page proof. They expect it to be out in the new year.'

'What is all this to do with what I said?'

'The forty-sixth psalm has *shake* and *speare* in it.'

'That is not possible. None would have it, this I knew. It would be seen as bombastic and overweening.'

'Tillotson, one of those charged with the overseeing of our emendations, said that the two words came nearer to the original than what they formerly had.'

'That is not possible.'

'He had never, I could see,' and Ben smiled sweetly, 'heard of the name Shakespeare.'

'Let us,' said Will, 'go and drink.'

2

ZARF.

Enderby came fighting awake with the word halfway down his nose. With too an unexpected and certainly premature homesickness for La Belle Mer in Tangiers, expressed in thirst for tea made with six Lipton sachets in the mug with the blazon CHICAGO – MY KIND OF TOWN. His men, Antonio, Manuel and the lad from Tetuan called Tetuani blowing on boiling lemon tea in glasses inserted in handled metal zarfs or zarfim. Windy Tangerine morning.

The mug had been given him by a Jewish visitor to Tangiers, citizen of that city full of wind, who claimed acquaintanceship with a Jewish novelist called Bellow, name appropriate to a windy city. Enderby did not read novels. Even less did he practise the craft of prose fiction, but he had published much earlier in the year a short or shortish story. This was in response to a Canadian university magazine's begging for free contributions, preferably money but prose acceptable. He had submitted a fantasy about Shakespeare's free contribution to the King James Bible. That was why he was on this aircraft now. They rode over an endless bed of dirty whipped cream. High above the wind.

He had had the fantasy in mind ever since the sneering response to his *Collected Poems* in the British literary press. Shakespeare must have suffered the same kind of self-pity, doubt as to validity of vocation and all the rest of it, reading sneers from MAs Oxon. and Cantab. in duodecimo summations of the proto-Elizabethan literary achievement, the greatness of Munday, Tibbs, Gough, Welkinshaw and other swollen poetas-

35

ters, bellowsed by bribed or sincerely stupid criticasters. But Shakespeare could comfort himself by stroking his coat of arms and thinking on the swelling of his acres and bags of malt stored up against the next eagerly awaited famine. He, Enderby, could not in honesty find a germane comfort in his proprietorship of a Tangerine beach restaurant with changing rooms for pustular bathers.

In the aircraft a film was proceeding. It was, to Enderby, a silent film, for he had no headset as it had been called. He had been unwilling to pay 3 dollars 50 for the hire of the apparatus. In front and behind and to his left fellow passengers were undergoing each the private experience of hearing shouts and screams and the roar of flames as people were burned alive in an aircraft. It was a very indiscreet sort of film.

He would, he had said a month ago, addressing himself to a bloody shave, write no more verse. There was nothing else to write about. Yet here he was being commissioned to write not only verse but mock Tudor dialogue. A musical play on the career of William Shakespeare to celebrate, for the commission was inevitably American, the second American centennial conjoined with the three hundred and sixtieth anniversary of Shakespeare's death. It was not immediately clear what connection there could be between the death of a poet and the birth of a sort of nation, and Enderby puzzled fuzzily, as the burning aircraft struck the sea and presumably sizzled, about the arithmology of the conjunction. 360. It was well known that Thomas Jefferson, Augustan voice of liberty, had possessed 360 slaves. With 360 degrees a wheel came full circle. With two centuries you came full circle twice. It was all a lot of nonsense.

The film ended with certain people wet but rescued and then an endless rolling list of the film's perpetrators. Plastic blinds were pushed up and the cabin's ports let in sick light. All that dirty whipped cream. The man next to Enderby removed his headset and said:

'It was about this aircraft catching fire.'

'So I gathered,' Enderby said. 'A visual experience really.'

'I guess you could say that.' He was middle-aged, overfed, and his face flaunted peeling shards of scarfskin from, Enderby divined, exposure to the Spanish sun. The plane came from

36

Madrid. 'Guess,' he said, doing it with thickish fingers, 'I'd better adjust my watch to Chicago time.'

'My sort of town,' Enderby said.

'Is that right?'

'No, it's on this mug I have. For tea, that is.'

'Is that right?'

If he could have tea now, *real* tea, not the gnatpiss they prepared in that sort of galley there, he would have it with seven sachets, not six. As you got older you required your tea stronger, that was laid down somewhere. Enderby was getting old.

Not too old though, by George or by God, probably the same person, for some new small adventure. The world of the theatre or theater, by Godgeorge. America, by Gorge. He had gone, on receiving the letter, to his private quarters to look up Indiana in *Everyman's Encyclopaedia*, an oldish edition but, if the place at all existed, it would probably be there. It seemed at first not only there but very big and exotic, but it was India he was looking at. Indiana was, he found, just under India House, demolished 1861. N. central state of the USA, generally known as the Hoosier State. 91 per cent of total area farmland. Iron, glass, carriages, railroad cars, woollens, etc. Climate remarkably equable. Leading cities Indianapolis, Fort Wayne, South Bend, Evansville, Gary. Terrebasse not mentioned. The theatre in Terrebasse was called the Peter Brook Theater. He looked up in another volume Brook, Peter, but found no information. Some local villainous benefactor requiring memorialization perhaps. He said to the man next to him, hands on lap, watch adjusted:

'Hoosier.'

'Pardon me?'

'The Hoosier State.'

'That's what they call Indiana.'

'Why?'

'If you're from Indiana you're a Hoosier.'

No help there. He did not much like the sound of it. It sounded like the kind of jeer which might well greet, in a territory nearly all farms, a sensible stage presentation of the main facts of the life of a major poet.

The man reimposed his headset, get his money's worth, and

turned a little black dial on his seat arm. 'Foog,' he said with disgust.

'Pardon me?', this being apparently the right mode of request for repetition or elucidation.

'This guy says they're going to play a foog.'

'Fugue,' Enderby said with energy. 'Tyranny of the verse line. They say there's no rhyme for fugue. But in song there is. Another fugue, oh, please no, Hugo. You can rhyme anything in a song. In Massachusetts ah took the pledge. Each glass ah chew sets mah teeth on edge.'

'That's it, I guess,' the man said; not listening, turning the black knob to, Enderby supposed, something infugal.

Enderby took from the inside pocket of his decent though oldish clerical grey suit the letter from Ms Grace Hope, a name he could not believe. Hollywood agent mixed up for some shady reason with play promotion. Understood from Toronto office Enderby only man who could do it. On strength of Toronto-published work called *Will and Testament*. Enderby occasionally feared that the letter, having been maliciously typed in disappearing ink, might emerge from that pocket a folded blank. Fare and expenses recoverable, but must pay them himself first. Artistic director, Angus Toplady, was, he being a director, to direct. Long creative discussions required, meaning everybody wanted to be called creator nowadays. Consequence of death of God or something. Music to come from pencil of Mike Silversmith, valued client of Ms Hope. It was all there, though stained with strong tea and fried eggyolk and hamfat, breakfast reading. Frank Merely, London associate at World Creation in Soho Square, arrange contract. Enderby doubted the reality of all these names.

Well, the place would continue languidly to run in his absence. A home, after all, for Antonio, Manuel and Tetuani. They were good boys really, despite their kif and buggery, as honest as could be reasonably expected in a Moroccan ambience. A sufficiency of farinaceous meals in the kitchen, a doss down wherever it was convenient to lay the night's mattresses, the odd sly nip, though *haram* for Tetuani, from the bottles behind the bar. With their master away they would all sleep on his floorbed, covered with sheepskins. On his return they would still be there tiredly sweeping and frying, though reporting no profit with triumphant teeth, since no profit was better than a loss.

A beefy voice announced through static an impending descent to O'Hare Airport. There Enderby must find an aircraft that would take him to Indiana. There he was to be picked up by some minion of Toplady, who was possibly a debased descendant of the author of *Rock of Ages*, and be driven to a Holiday Inn, though not for a holiday. Having seen on Spanish television a film with Bing Crosby about the pioneering of this hotel chain, Enderby had an image of a large shack of decayed wood with snow swirling about it. But this was autumn, or the fall, and, the weather of Indiana being equable, there would probably be no snow.

A silly asthenic corn queen came round collecting headsets. The neighbour of Enderby gave his up and then turned to Enderby as if, he relieved of the responsibility of using it, the two of them could settle to an urgent colloquy necessarily deferred. 'This your first visit?' he said.

'To where?'

'To the States.'

'Well, yes, though not, I assure you, for lack of previous invitations. I should have gone to New York to become a professor for a time. A consequence of *The Wreck of the Deutschland*,* you know. It was a question of one or the other. So I chose this. More creative than Creative Writing, if you see what I mean.'

'Is that right?'

'More or less. A blasphemous cinematic adaptation of a great mystical poem, and I was involved, though in a way unwittingly. I didn't intend it should turn out the way it did.'

'Is that right?'

'Very much so.' Enderby had not been speaking English for a long time. It struck him that he was speaking it now as from a book. He must do something about making it more colloquial. 'Putting the boot in,' he said. 'The Nazis shagging coifed nuns. Violence and violation. Too much of that around.'

'You can say that again.'

'Too much of that around.'

*See *The Clockwork Testament.*

39

This man did not, as might be expected from even an enforced companionship of several hours, assist Enderby on his entrance to a strange land. He was quick to get away with no valediction. Enderby was on his own. O'Hare Airport seemed very large. The immigration officials seemed to let everyone in, even Americans, very grudgingly and only after looking up every name in a big book like a variorum edition of something. But Enderby was eventually permitted to have his luggage examined with great thoroughness. The examiner of luggage was a hard man in outdoor middle age.

'What's this?'

'A kind of denture adhesive or tooth glue. A Spanish product. For affixing dentures to the gums or, in the case of the upper prosthesis, to the hard palate.'

'What?'

Enderby was roughly prevented from demonstrating. The stomach tablets came under closer scrutiny. The customs officer took samples of each in little vials.

'For dyspepsia,' Enderby said, and demonstrated the sonic aspects of the condition.

'You mean you got a bad stomach?'

'Only after eating. The food on the plane was bloody awful. They warm everything up, as you know.'

'Why,' the officer asked with great earnestness, 'are you entering the United States?'

'To work in what you people call a theater.'

'You an actor?'

'I am a poet. I am Enderby the poet.'

'*What?*'

'If you want proof,' Enderby said, coldly pointing to his messed up shirts, 'there are my poems.'

The officer picked up the book with the tips of his fingers. He opened it. 'Don't make much sense to me,' he said.

'Every man to his trade. What you're doing with people's luggage doesn't make much sense to, ah, myself. So there we are.'

'Listen, fella,' the man said quietly but rudely, 'I got my job to do, right?'

'And I mine.'

'There might be narcotics in those things you got there for your stomach, right?'

40

'Not right. I never touch them. Seen too much of the effects. But I thought we were talking about poetry.' The people behind Enderby were looking at their watches and muttering for Chrissake, as in an American novel. Enderby was growlingly let go. He walked long and in some pain through several miles of airport building. Twinges in the left calf, cholesterol buildup. There were a lot of irritable people, also shops and restaurants. He saw many copies of his own mug on sale. When he came to the place where it said INDIANAPOLIS he was exhausted. He would have given anything for a mug, CHICAGO MY KIND OF or not, of very strong tea. He compromised with a couple or so capsules of Estomag, chewing them vigorously. An eager shifty thin little man in jeans and a dirty singlet came up to him and said: 'Hi.' He had a shock of wirewool hair but was not Hamitic. Nor Japhetic either. 'Mike Silversmith,' he said.

'How did you know it was. Recognition, I mean.'

'You opened that bag to take out that stuff that's all round your mouth. There's a book in it with your name on.'

This was not the kind of assumption that Enderby liked. People with names like Gomez or Krumpacker could conceivably be comforting their journeys with the *Collected Poems*. Conceivably, only just. Enderby wiped his mouth with his hand. 'The composer,' he said.

'Right.' He sat without invitation next to Enderby. 'I got these cassettes in my bag here already. They'll knock you. "To be or not to be in love with you". Then there's "Tomorrow and Tomorrow". '

'And Tomorrow,' added Enderby. 'It's three times. But it's me who's doing the words.' Colloquial was coming nicely back to him. Anger was paying its first visit. He had thought it might be like this.

'You and Shakespeare,' Silversmith said. ' "To be or not to be in love with you". You take it from there. But you hear the tune first.'

'How about the words I've written already and which, presumably, you've seen. Already,' he added.

'Never get in the charts with them.'

They were summoned aboard by a man in a powder blue blazer.

'What,' asked Enderby with care, 'kind of an orchestra do

you propose?' A black child clinging to its necessarily black mother's hand looked up at him. They were shuffling aboard. Silversmith was in front of Enderby. 'Viols,' proposed Enderby, 'recorders, cornetts, tabors. Authenticity.'

But Silversmith was addressing the imbecilic stewardess as honey. He knew her, he had come this way before. Or perhaps not. Enderby was obliged to sit next to Silversmith and then to put on a headset attached to a Japanese cassette recorder which Silversmith eagerly took from a scuffed bag. 'Listen,' Silversmith said. Enderby heard a voice, Silversmith's from the sound of it, scrannelling perverted words from *Hamlet* while a guitar thrummed chords.

> 'To be or not to be
> In love with you,
> To spend my entire life
> Hand in glove with you.'

Then the voice, having no more words, lahed and booped on to the end, which was the same as the beginning. Enderby carefully fastened his seatbelt. He as carefully freed his ears of the noise and the foam rubber. Silversmith said:

'You take it from there, right?'

'Wrong,' Enderby said. 'If you think I'm going to permit William Shakespeare to sing inanities like that – '

'What's that word?'

'Inanities. It's a desecration.'

Silversmith sighed. 'I can see,' he said, 'it's going to be like I told Gus Toplady it was going to be. You got too many long words in that thing you sent him. You got to consider the public.'

'I've got to consider Shakespeare.'

'Ah, Jesus,' Silversmith said.

'After all,' Enderby said, 'we were all warned.'

'Warned about what?'

'About disturbing his bones. There's a curse waiting.'

'Yeah, sure,' Silversmith said, and he pretended to go to sleep. The aircraft started to bear them to Indianapolis.

3

'More of a prologue or induction really,' Enderby said.

'In what?' somebody crossly asked.

'Come, come,' Enderby said in an unwisely schoolmasterly tone. 'You all remember your *Taming of the Shrew*.'

This resident company, lounging in deplorable rags in a kind of classroom complete with blackboard, did not seem to like being instructed in the terminology of drama by a man in a decent, though old, clerical grey suit. Their director was not dressed like that. He was too old, though, for the coûture and coiffure he affected. Dirty grey sculpted sideburns. Silk shirt of black covered with sharpnosed Greek heroes in gold in postures of harmless aggression. Grey chest hairs and dangling medallions. Chinos stained at the crotch. Bare feet in fawn suede cowboy boots. Enderby felt he himself was there as for the reading of a will, which in a sense he was.

The people not there were the people who should have been there. But Shakespeare was to be played by a film actor who was the husband of Ms Grace Hope, and he was making a film. The dark lady who was to play the Dark Lady was completing a nightclub engagement. *Hamlet* without the prince, Enderby had quipped. Gus Toplady had morosely replied that he had tried it in Minneapolis at the Tyrone Guthrie but it had not really worked. Hamlet off stage all the time, Rosencrantz and Guildenstern eavesdropping on inaudible soliloquy. What's he say now? He say he not know whether he live or die but he use too many big words. Toplady had done a nude *Macbeth* somewhere. He appeared to have little confidence in Enderby. Enderby reciprocated with all his heartburn.

'Shakespeare,' Enderby said, 'is dying. His ageing wife and two daughters sit by his bed, the wife audibly jingling two pennies. These are to put on his eyes when he shall finally close them.'

'Why?' asked a girl whom Enderby knew to be Toplady's mistress.

'The custom in those days. These are not what ah you would call pennies. Not cents I mean. Big pennies. English ones.'

'Okay,' Toplady said without compassion. 'He's dying. Forget the pennies.'

'You can't,' Enderby said. 'Shakespeare says: "Ah, I hear you jingling your pennies to put on my eyes. Do not fret, wife. I shall not keep you waiting long." Then, though it's still April, he hears the song of boys and girls bringing in the May. They sing the ah following:

'Bringing the maypole home,
Bringing the maypole home,
Bringing the maypole home,
Bringing the maypole home.'

'A deathless lyric,' Toplady said.

'There's more to it than that,' Enderby said, red. 'It goes on:

'Custom has blessed this strange festivity,
Licensing every gross proclivity,
Here's the year's nativity,
Here is life, let's live it.
To sin it is no sin
When spring is coming in.'

He looked round for a positive response, but there was none, except of vague incredulity. He pushed on sturdily:

'In his dying delirium he sees the mayers prancing about the deathchamber, his younger self and Anne Hathaway among them. He says: "Thus it began. She overbore me in a wood. Needed a husband, even though one ten years younger. Susannah there born but six months after the marriage." Himself dying and his surrounding family fade into blackness, and the younger Shakespeare, whom we will call Will for brevity, is sitting in a chair nursing his son Hamnet.'

44

'What happens to the singing and dancing?' asked somebody.

'That is ah sung and danced off. But this is another May and Will hears the song in the distance. He hugs his little son and sings to him as follows:

> 'Little son,
> When I look at thee
> I am filled with won-
> Der such wonder should be.
> Part of me yet no part of me,
> Wholly good yet the wood of my tree.
> If I could
> I would live to see
> Fulfilled in me
> The man that I can never be,
> Born to property,
> Richly clad retainers about thee.
> Hawk on hand,
> You survey your land,
> Your acres shining in the summer's gold
> And I behold
> The glory of a name
> Restored to fame
> It had of old.
> Little son,
> If these things should be
> And I die before they are granted to thee,
> Think of me as he who carved them
> From the wood
> For the wood of my tree.'

There was a silence. Toplady said to Silversmith, who lay on the floor: 'Mike?' Silversmith pronounced:

'I say what I said already.' Toplady said with cold eyes to Enderby:

'Go on. But cut out the lyrics.'

'But the whole of this ah induction is done practically entirely in song.'

'Go on.'

'Well,' Enderby said, 'Will goes to the window and looks up at the clear night sky. He sees, but we do not see, Cassiopeia's

45

Chair, a constellation in the shape of an inverted W, the initial of his name. He sings to it.'

'Ah Jesus,' said Silversmith from the floor.

'He sings to it as follows:

> 'My name in the sky
> Burning for ever,
> Fame fixed by fate
> Never to die.
> At least
> I feast on that dream,
> The gleam of gold, my fortunes mounting high.
> To render my deed
> More than pure fancy,
> On lonely roads I must proceed,
> My one companion a dream,
> A seemly vision only I espy!
> My name in the sky.

'But then his wife Anne appears and sings a contrary song which combines in counterpoint with Will's:

> 'Will o' the wisp,
> A foolish fire,
> Leads fools to fall
> In mud and mire.
> Better by far
> The fire at home,
> Smoke in the rafter,
> Lamb's wool and laughter – '

'What,' Toplady's mistress asked, 'does lamb's wool have to do with it?'

'Lamb's wool,' Enderby authoritatively defined, 'was an Elizabethan drink for cold weather, consisting of heated ale mixed with the pounded pulp of roasted crab apples, which fragments floated in the ale like the wool of lambs in a high wind. Seasoned with nutmeg, cinnamon, ginger and cloves. Highly fortifying.'

'You'd have to have a programme note,' said a bearded youth, 'or some guy standing there to stop the song and explain it.'

'Push on,' Toplady said in the tone of one who leads a toiling party through a high wind.

46

'Anne finishes the song:

> 'Will o' the wisp,
> Do not desire
> To follow fame,
> That foolish fire.
> Better by far
> The fire at home,
> Fresh dawn on waking
> And fresh bread baking.
> A will o' the wisp
> Should not aspire
> To be a star.'

'Mike?'
'Like I said already.'
'But,' pleaded Enderby, 'they both hear approaching song. It is the company of players known as the Queen's Men. They have been playing in Stratford and are now leaving it, with their property carts and clopping horses. The troupe sings:

> 'The Queen's Men,
> The Queen's Men,
> Not beer-and-bread-and-beans men
> But fine men,
> Wine men,
> Music-while-we-dine men.
> The Queen's Men,
> The Queen's Men,
> Of-more-than-ample-means men,
> Are off now,
> Doff, bow,
> We will come again,
> The Queeeeeeen's Men.'

Enderby prolonged the long vowel in a gesture of song: 'Hearing it, Will says: "By God, I will go with them. I will become a player and eke write plays – " '
'Why does he go eek?' a fat frizzy girl in crimson asked.
'Eke means also,' learned Enderby said. 'Cognate with German *auch*. But he can say also if that is what is, ah, desired.'
'That is, ah, desired,' the girl said.

'He says to his little son: "I will be back with fine gifts for Hamnet. And eke Susannah and Judith. And eke their mother." Or, if that is still desired, also. Anne sings her Will o' the Wisp song and Will his Cassiopeia song again, and both are in counterpoint to the song of the Queen's Men. The scene ends. The curtain goes up almost at once on Elizabethan London in the full flush of victory over the Spaniards. A song is sung which begins with a kind of ah fart – '

'Your first job,' Toplady said, 'was to find out about the stage. This stage has no curtains. Go and look at it sometime. No curtains.'

'Except for someone,' Silversmith said obscurely from the floor.

'A sort of er fart,' Enderby went on, 'like this:

> 'Prrrrrrrp
> We ha' done for the Don,
> Clawed off his breeches
> And rent every stitch he's
> Had on – '

'Right,' Toplady said to the company, 'you can see a lot of work has to be done yet, and our friend here says that this is only what he calls an induction – '

'Shakespeare too,' Enderby cut in. 'You all know your *Taming of the*.'

'Watch noticeboard for next reading call. Okay,' dismissively. To Enderby he said: 'You and me and Mike have to talk. In ten minutes in my office.'

'You,' Enderby said, 'do not appear to like the project.'

'I like any project that has a fart in hell's chance of working. This project we've got to do. There's money gone into it from Mrs Schoenbaum. She wants it and to Mrs Schoenbaum you don't say no. But we don't do the project the way you see the project or think you see it.' He breathed on Enderby and exuded a memory of breakfast blueberry pancakes. 'Ten minutes in my office.' Both he and Enderby had to leave by the same door, but it was if they were to exit by opposed wings. Silversmith remained on the floor. Enderby said harshly to him:

48

'Good friend for Jesus' sake forbear
To dig the dust enclosed here.
Blest be the man who spares these stones
But curst be he who moves my bones.'

'That too,' Silversmith said, 'is a shitty lyric.' Enderby was constrained, though silently, to agree with him. He then lost himself in the bowels of the theater among shut cabin doors, fat heating pipes, growling engines. A big place, he concluded, having passed twice the same boilersuited men playing cards. At length he found himself in the wings of a stage and he timidly ventured onto the stage itself which, true, had no curtains and jutted far into an auditorium far too large for the town of Terrebasse but not for playgoers from the state capital, which was near. Less shyly, he moved downstage in the dusk mitigated by a working light and tried certain lines:
'By God, I will follow them to London and make my fortune there, acting plays and eke writing them.' Terrible. A man who now appeared in the wings with a hamburger seemed to think so too, for he clapped faintly.

Enderby went down to the auditorium and through it, uphill, to doors which led to a wide corridor. Then there were stairs and he came to the administrative area, where girls and grown women were typing. He was somewhat late. Toplady glowered from his open office. Silversmith was already lying on the floor. Toplady's office was full of framed posters of his triumphs in high colour and fancy lettering. Toplady drank coffee from a paper cup and so, with some loss of the substance, did Silversmith. No coffee was offered to Enderby but a chair was. Toplady sat behind his desk. He said:
'What's the story?'
'The story, yes. Shakespeare, or Will as we may call him for brevity's sake, said that already, sorry, leaves wife and children in Stratford and goes to London. He sees how the Londoners like violent sports like bearbaiting and beheadings at Tyburn, so he writes the most violent play ever written. I see you presumably know it, Mr Ladysmith, since a poster there says you once directed it. Not a good play. In fact,' he said daringly, 'a lousy one.'
'Go on.'

49

'This leads him to the *Henry VI* plays and the friendship of the Earl of Southampton and at least acquaintanceship with the Earl of Essex, who wants to be king of England. Then there is *Richard III*, which leads him to the Dark Lady. She sees the play and falls for Burbage who plays the lead, and wants him to come to her bed with the announcement at the door that Richard III is here. But Will gets there first and is at his work when the announcement comes and says tell him William the Conqueror comes before Richard III.'

The anecdote made Enderby smile but the two others remained gloomily watching. He continued:

'The Earl of Southampton takes the Dark Lady away from him and he falls into depression and whoring and drinking. You could have a song about that,' he suggested.

'Depression, whoring and drinking,' Silversmith sang from the floor.

'And then comes the news that his son Hamnet is very sick. He rushes to Stratford to find his boy dead and being buried. But he becomes a gentleman. Too late, too late, alas. This,' Enderby saw fit now to explain, 'is a play about guilt.'

'Go on.'

'End of first act. Second act Will is involved in Essex rebellion through putting on *Richard II*, which appears to justify usurpation. He sees Essex beheaded and fears he will be beheaded himself. But the Queen tells him to stay out of the big world of politics. He is a little man, she says. He goes home to Stratford and looks after his land and sues everybody in the manner of a country gentleman. Then he dies. A brief outline only.' Silence. 'It could be expanded.' Silence. 'A lot of things happen really. Marlowe, Ben Jonson. Sex and murder.' Silence. 'No limit to dramatic possibilities. Gentlemen,' he added.

'You know what this is really about?' Toplady eventually said.

'Of course he could have syphilis, if that would help at all. He probably did have. Marvellous description of symptoms in *Timon of Athens*. Read it sometime. Nose dropping off, voice getting hoarse and so on. Everybody had syphilis in those days. America's gift to Europe. All the world's a tertiary stage, he might have said. I don't know why I'm telling you all this.'

'What I said,' Toplady said more loudly though untruthfully, 'is that this play is about its two stars.'

Enderby coldly answered his cold stare. 'You mean,' he said, 'like the *Guide Michelin*?' He had no confidence whatsoever in Toplady.

'I mean,' Toplady said, 'Pete Oldfellow and April Elgar. They're the stars. You'd better believe it. You can't put April on for a single scene and then shovel her off like dogshit. Once she's there she's there. You see that?'

'I don't,' Enderby said, 'think I know the lady. The name, of course. Elgar's a great name. But I thought the family had died out. Worcestershire, as you know.'

'April is black,' reproved the voice from the floor. 'April is only Worcester in the sauce sense. April is the hottest property. April is tabasco.' Enderby listened with unwilling approval. This was pure poetry.

'April Elgar,' Toplady explained, 'is a great singing star. You don't seem to realize what's on here. We take this show to Broadway by way of here and Toronto and Boston. It could run for ever.'

'Why,' Enderby asked, with seeming irrelevance, 'did you pick on me?'

'Had to pick on somebody,' Toplady said. 'We didn't want one of these professors. Mrs Schoenbaum has to be convinced she's getting what she asked for. Meaning Shakespeare. Now get this first act ready. Shakespeare comes from Stratford bringing his kid with him.'

'Hamnet? But he didn't. Hamnet stayed with his mother.'

'You may,' Toplady said, 'think I'm an ignorant bastard, but I know what I don't know. More important, I know what *you* don't know. What you don't know is what really happened. Okay, who's to say he didn't bring his kid with him? He brings his kid with him but he protects him from the dirty world. He puts this dirty world on the stage. The Dark Lady comes into his life. He neglects his kid and his kid dies – plague, mugging, falls from a scaffold, gets roughed by a mad horse, gang rape, anything will do. So, right, you can have your guilt and remorse or whatever the hell it is.' He scooped the gift towards Enderby with a Toledo dagger Enderby assumed was used as a paper-knife. 'She leaves him for this other guy, the Earl of Southampton or Sussex. She's got ambitions, right?'

'Essex. But look here – '

'Who cares what sex, right, but she's back in Act Two. In Act Two Shakespeare wants his son back so he turns him into Hamlet, and Shakespeare plays the Ghost.'

'You got that from – '

'Never mind where I got it. The rebellion's because she wants to be queen. She only gets to be queen in Shakespeare's dream. She becomes Cleopatra. When he's sick and losing his teeth and getting old, she drops him. But she's really his mooz.'

'His what?'

'His inspiration. Fella, you have enough to be getting on with. But remember we don't have all that much time.'

'Right,' came, unurgently, from the floor.

'My title,' Enderby said. With great reluctance he had to admit to a faint admiration for Toplady. Horribly blasphemous and obscene though it was, he seemed to know what he wanted.

'Your title is out. Who wants to see a musical called *Whoever Hath Thy Will*? There's a lot round here can't say *th*. I thought of *Goats and Monkeys*. You know where that comes from.' He nodded up at a poster advertising his production of *Othello*, in which everybody in the blown-up photograph of turmoil on Cyprus seemed, except for Othello, who, in his general's uniform, looked like Patton, to be black. 'That's our working title, anyway. Something else may turn up. There's a room and a typewriter along there. You'd best get moving.'

Enderby humbly obeyed, or at least got out of there. Silversmith said: 'Your first lyric is the Tomorrow and Tomorrow one. Get it finished today.'

4

In the dark bar of the Holiday Inn, whisky sour before him,
Enderby wrote a lyric:

> Give the people what they wish:
> Something trite and tawdry,
> Balladry and bawdry –
> Give the people what they wish.
> Give the groundlings what they crave:
> Bombast and unreason,
> Dog and bitch in season,
> Prophecies of treason
> Rising from the grave.
> Pillaging and ravishing and burning,
> Royal heads and maidenheads
> Presented on a dish,
> In a pie.
> Let them eat their stinking fish –
> What they find delicious
> Soon will seem pernicious.
> When the time's propitious
> That diet will cloy,
> They will come to enjoy
> What I wish
> What I wish
> What Iiiiiiiiiiiiiii
> Wish.

Let that bloody Silverlady or Topsmith try that one, see what
his rhythmical sense was like. Enderby began to sketch the
dialogue that followed. He preferred to work here than in the

room they had given him. Too many people kept looking in to see how he was getting on. The mistress of Silvertop came twice to giggle. She was a thin long girl with red hair who was to play Queen Elizabeth. Enderby had set his scene in a brothel. Will in the dark with a spot on him while singing. Lights come up to disclose whores in undress. Henslowe with his account book. He frowns on Will and waves him away.

'State your requirements to the madam. She will be down anon.'

'No no no. It is you I want. Or him there, your son-in-law. Master Alleyn, that is.' For Ned Alleyn has appeared, putting his doublet on.

'I know you, I think,' Henslowe says. 'You owe me fourpence.'

'I owe nothing, not to any man. Forgive my seeking you here. I have a play.'

'Ah, sweet Jesus, will they never give up?'

'Listen. You may have it for nothing if it runs not more than three afternoons.'

'A prodigy,' Alleyn says. 'He owes no money and he gives things away.'

'Listen. I'll be brief. The scene is Rome. A barbarian empress is captured by the Romans but allowed her liberty. Hating the Romans nevertheless, she urges her sons to ravish a noble matron.'

'Why?' Alleyn asks.

'A sort of revenge. Listen. The sons kill the matron's husband, then ravish her on her husband's dead body, which serves in manner of a bloody mattress. Then, that the wretched woman may not tell, they cut out her tongue.'

'Go on. To hear costs nothing.'

'That she may not write the names of her ravishers, they cut off her hands as well.'

'Dirty stuff,' says Henslowe. 'Go on.'

'But she takes a stick between her two stumps and then scratches her ravishers' names on the earth. Then her father avenges her.'

'Ah' from both.

'He kills the sons and he grinds up their bones to a flour.

With this he makes a coffin of pastry. The filling is the cooked flesh of the two sons.'

'Indigestible,' says Alleyn. 'Let me see your script.'

'More indigestible than Tyburn hangings and quarterings? Then he invites the mother to a cannibalistic feast. There is also a black villain that gets the Gothic empress with child – a black child.'

' "He cuts their throats – He kills her – He stabs the empress – He stabs Titus – He stabs Saturninus – ".' Alleyn riffles through.

'And the Moor, a sort of black Machiavelli, he is buried up to his waist and left to starve.'

'Delectable,' says Alleyn, and he declaims:

> 'Ah, why should wrath be mute and fury dumb?
> I am no baby, I, that with base prayers
> I should repent the evils I have done.
> Ten thousand worse than ever yet I did
> Would I perform, if I might have my will.
> If one good deed in all my life I did,
> I do repent it from my very soul.'

So then the lights go out on that side of the stage, and on the other side the lights go up, those same final words of Aaron the Moor sounding again through the theatre, electronic blessing, as a ballet of stabbers and ravishers and poisoners prances to a music of screams and groans. Boys carrying publicity posters – HENRY VI I II & III – RICHARD III – thread through the dancers while Will, downstage centre, repeats his song. He makes way for Alleyn as Richard Crookback, who delivers a bloody speech. Lights go up on previously darkened segment to show the Dark Lady with her duenna, rich brown flesh and diamonds and crimson brocade, watching and listening intently. A note is passed to Alleyn as he exits. All this might do very well. Enderby stopped scribbling on his yellow legal pad. If they could get somebody to do better let them bloody well get on with it. He raised his empty glass to himself and also to the shortskirted blonde matron who was waiting on. He deserved another of those.

He had, he had to confess, given in to those two in some measure. The travelstained Warwickshire yokel, snotnosed son held by the hand, gawking in a London street. Growling bear led off to its baiting. A severed head or two gawking back at Will from gatespikes. Bosom-showing wenches. Hucksters. A bit like a dirtied-up opening for *Dick Whittington*. And then Will sings to Hamnet:

> Tomorrow and tomorrow and tomorrow –
> That makes three.
> The first tomorrow is for me.
> The second tomorrow – we.
> The third tomorrow – thee.
> I start with my poetic fame,
> I then restore the family name,
> And last of all I see
> Thee –
> Sir Hamnet, Lord Hamnet
> The day after the day after tomorrow.
> I pledge that these things shall be.

Terrible, but the music was terrible. Henslowe follows his growling bear. Will follows Henslowe. Good idea: Hamnet, left outside the brothel, finds his way in, seeing lust and bosoms. The beginning of his corruption. Two first scenes there in, as they said, the bag. The company could start rehearsing.

Enderby looked at his watch. Time to ask somebody at the front desk to seek him a taxi. He had to go to dinner at Mrs Schoenbaum's. Toplady, thank God, would not be there: there was a play on and he had to give his troupe confidence by glaring at them from the wings. The play was some libellous nonsense about the Salvation Army by a dead German named Brecht. Silversmith had taken a flying, literally, visit to New York to superintend what he called the pressing of an album, old-fashioned phrase recalling the crushing to death of flowers in young ladies' commonplace books.

He got a taxi with small difficulty. 1102 Sycamore Street. What's that number again, mister? The driver, a white man with Silversmith wire-wool hair, seemed to be, as they said here, stoned. He growled all the time like Henslowe's bear. 1102. Ain't never heard of that number. I can assure you it does exist. What's that you say, mister, and so on. There were no sycamores. Sumachs, rather, and a kind of hornbeam or

56

carpinus betulus. The driver seemed dissatisfied with his tip. He looked at his ensilvered palm as though Enderby had spat into it.

Enderby was let in by a muttering black man in a white jacket. Mrs Schoenbaum was there in the hallway to greet him. 'Mr Elderly? We are so honoured,' honored, really. Enderby shyly took in riches. Daubs on the walls which must be what were known as rich men's impressionists, cost millions. He knew that Mr Schoenbaum was dead from making money. Mrs Schoenbaum was clearly enjoying her widowhood. She wore a kind of harem dress of silk trousers and brocaded sort of cutdown caftan. Her silver hair was frozen into a photographed stormtossed effect, clicked into sempiternal tempestuousness on a Wuthering Heights of the American imagination. Her eyelids were gold-dusted and her lips white-lacquered. Her nose looked as though its natural butt had been surgically cut off. She took Enderby by the hand and led him into a salon with more daubs discreetly lighted. Enderby tottered and then recovered on bearskins laid on pine overpolished. 'Whoops,' Mrs Schoenbaum said, holding on to his hand. 'I'm sure,' she said, 'you know nobody here.' That was true. An evidently hired youth playing cocktail tripe on the Bechstein in a far corner sent over to Enderby a vulgar conspiratorial look. Enderby was introduced to two overweight men who got up from a couch as long as a barge with some difficulty. A middle-aged woman laden with beads did not, quite rightly, get up, but she fixed Enderby with eyes of hate. One overweight man was from the University of Indianapolis. The other seemed to be a lawyer or something shady of that kind. Enderby did not catch the names. 'Mrs Allegramente,' or something, said Mrs Schoenbaum, 'has promised to demonstrate her powers for us after dinner.' This Mrs Allegramente said, as Enderby boarded the couch and accepted a whisky with ice from the muttering black:

'When are you British going to quit Northern Ireland?'

'Which British do you mean?' Enderby asked with care.

'You colonizing British who are holding that poor country in a vice of disgusting tyranny.'

'Nothing to do with me. Ask Henry VIII and the Tudor founders of the Protestant plantation,' he jocularly added.

'I have already. A fat disgusting man with his mouth full of chicken bones.'

57

Mad. Good, he knew where he stood, lay rather. He too would have difficulty in getting up. The lawyer said:

'You just come over now then?'

'Well, yes. From Tangiers, where I live. I have ah severed connections with my country. Not its language, of course, nor its literature.'

'Mr Elderly,' Mrs Schoenbaum said, 'is a distinguished writer. He is doing this thing for us here. The life of Shakespeare set to music.'

'I guess so,' the lawyer said. He accepted more whisky. He and the black flunky grunted at each other. The distant pianist struck up a version of 'Greensleeves'. He knew what was wanted.

'Henry VIII himself wrote that,' Enderby blurted. 'A musician as well as a ah distinguished tyrant. Some of the words are obscene.'

'That figures,' Mrs Allegramente said. The academic said:

'Mrs Schoenbaum has done a lot for William Shakespeare.' He gave out the full name as though Mrs Schoenbaum had, for good reasons perhaps of an ethical nature, ignored the rest of the family. But Mrs Schoenbaum at once discountenanced that supposition by saying:

'Well, like I always said, Irwin, that's only natural. I am,' she told Enderby, 'related to the Shakespeares. By marriage, of course.' Enderby nodded. These American women were very straightforward people, quick to disclose their madness. The men were a little slower. These here would, after a few more whiskies, give out their madness with a circumspection proper to the professions they practised. 'Not, that is, through Mr Schoenbaum, of course, whose family was from Germany, but through the Quineys.'

'Thomas Quiney,' prompt Enderby said. 'He married Judith Shakespeare on 10 February 1616. Shakespeare had only a couple of months of life left after that. The shock did his health no good. A low tavernkeeper already convicted of fornication. The tavern he kept was called the Cage, an appropriate name considering the poor girl's virtually incarcerated condition. A barmaid. Now the place is a place that sells hamburgers.'

'Is that so,' said rather than asked the lawyer. Mrs Schoenbaum seemed unabashed by the details. She said:

'The Quineys emigrated to America and married into the Greenwoods, which is my family.'

'Under the Grünbaum tree,' unwisely quoted Enderby, 'who loves to lie with me.'

'Well, Greenwood was not always the name, as you so er quickly devised. But I got back to the baum bit with my late husband.'

'A lovely man,' obituarized the lawyer.

'He called me Queenie,' Mrs Schoenbaum said, 'when he found out that's how Quiney was sometimes pronounced. He spent much time and money, Mr Elderly, on my geneography. He was deeply interested. But my real name is Laura.'

'And my real name,' Enderby said, 'is Enderby. Not Elderly.'

'We're all getting on a little,' said the academic called Irwin, 'except for our lovely hostess. And, of course, for Mrs Allegramente.' The young man at the piano called across the room over his rolling chords the word shit. Mrs Schoenbaum said:

'There's no call for that language, Philip. My son,' she confided to Enderby. 'He is very unsociable.'

'He has a considerable social gift,' Enderby said. 'He er manages that superb instrument with great panache and er vivacity.'

'Do you have children, sir?' the lawyer asked in an accusatory manner. His thick eyebrows, Enderby now noticed, had been given, perhaps by art, a devilish upsweep at the outer edges. He had several chins.

'I think not,' Enderby said. 'Paternity, however, is said to be a legal fiction.'

'Surely, surely,' Mrs Schoenbaum seemed to soothe. 'And are they properly looking after you at the place where you are staying?'

'It is the Holiday Inn,' Enderby said. 'I cannot get tea. It's as bad as France with this dipping of bags into tepid water. I asked for one of their big coffee jugs to be filled with boiling water and for seven sachets to be steeped in it. They considered this to be British eccentricity.'

Mrs Allegramente, responding to the signal British, said: 'You better quit Northern Ireland right now if you know what's good for you. I can read the signs.'

'She has great gifts,' Mrs Schoenbaum said, 'as we shall see demonstrated after.'

'What they did,' Enderby continued, 'was to put *three* sachets in a jug which already contained what they call coffee. The manager was not helpful. So I bought my own apparatus.'

'You did, eh?' said the academic with uncalled-for animation. 'You went out and bought the wherewithal and now make tea of the required strength in your own room?'

'I most certainly did and do. A kind of kettle and a big mug. Condensed milk. A box of sachets from a store called CHEEP CHEEP with the recorded song of a canary playing all the time.'

'Is that so? Is that really so?' The academic's pisshued eyes glowed with interest. 'It's in the private sector that the major events of human life occur. Ah,' he said, 'here is Lucille.'

'My daughter,' Mrs Schoenbaum said. A girl with jeans and a tee-shirt came in saying hi to everyone. The tee-shirt had Shakespeare as bigfisted flying Superman on it with the legend WILL POWER. 'She is a dropout.'

Enderby assumed that the term, combining knockout and coughdrop, was a slangy tribute to beauty not at once apparent. 'She certainly is,' he said. She advertised the lipoid virtues of what he had heard called junkfood, presumably food for junkies, whom, living in Tangiers, he knew all about. A girl greasy as though basted. He was glad when she said she had to split. She had things to do with her friends, to whom too she would say hi. She took her big worn blue arse away. She collided with the black servant who came in to say they could all eat if they wanted. Mrs Schoenbaum told him that Philip would not be eating with them, an aspect of his unsociability. The black man could give Philip a sandwich and a coke. The black man seemed to demur and said things unintelligible but certainly rebellious in tone. Everybody helped each other to get out of the couch barge. Enderby slithered on wool and high polish. The black man cackled.

The dining room was like a great tomb with votive flowers and candles. Enderby could not see into its corners but he observed over his head an untenanted minstrels' gallery. There were highlighted what he took to be Cézannes, bad paintings of apples and bottles. 'Paella,' Mrs Schoenbaum announced,

60

pronouncing the double clear L as a single dark one. 'In honour of our guest who lives where it is part of the kwee zeen.'

'Never see it in Tangiers,' Enderby said. 'Couscous country.'

'Is that so,' the lawyer said. The dish that the black man grousingly put on the table was all shells and bits of rubber and soggy rice. There was chlorinated water but no wine. You were supposed to bring your highball in with you. Enderby had finished his. He had been placed next to Mrs Allegramente. She now started again on the theme of suffering Ulster. Enderby was fed up. He said:

'Get this straight. I was brought up an English Catholic. I've no time for those bloody Orangemen there. They say an Orangeman's dinner consists of roast spuds, boiled spuds, chips and croquettes.'

'Is that so.'

'Pudgy bastards who discharge their carbohydrated energy in gross tribalism. No time for the sods. So hand the place over to the IRA for all I care. But it's no business of the Yanks.'

Mrs Schoenbaum was a polite hostess. She ignored her British guest's snarl and said: 'I hear great things of our project. I understand that things are going really well.'

'Conflicts,' Enderby said, and spat a bit of shell onto his fork end. 'They will all be resolved. This was your idea, or so I'm credibly informed.'

'It was the idea,' Mrs Schoenbaum said, 'of the Bard himself. Ask Mrs Allegramente.' Enderby choked. 'He spoke from the Happy House and said he was delighted that America had achieved two hundred years of free nationhood. He wished to be associated in song and dance with our celebrations.' Enderby looked darkly, in the dark, at Mrs Allegramente, who looked, though chewing something unchewable, darkly back. 'After dinner we shall tune in to him again. It's a great privilege,' said Mrs Schoenbaum.

'He will not speak to the sceptical,' Mrs Allegramente said.

'What,' Enderby asked, 'is this Happy House you spoke of?'

'The mansion of the blessed,' Mrs Schoenbaum said. 'He is with his fellow writers. He sent greetings from John Steinbeck, who would not speak for himself.'

'I met Steinbeck,' Enderby said, 'when he was given, unjustly I thought and still think, the Nobel, oh I don't know

61

though when you consider some of these dago scribblers who get it, think it was an unjust bestowal. There was a party for him given by Heinemann in London. I asked him what he was going to do with the prize money and he said: *Fuck off.*' Before he could apologize, the academic said:

'Don't apologize. *Oratio recta.* Such a response I find deeply interesting. The private sector of a man's life.'

'This was in public,' Enderby said. 'I apologize for what he said,' he said to Mrs Schoenbaum. Mrs Schoenbaum, who evidently heard worse from her children, inclined queenlily. 'I trust,' he said with swimming brain, 'the er bard keeps his language clean.'

'He will not speak to sceptics,' Mrs Allegramente said.

'What kind of sceptics do you have in mind? People who believe his works were written by the gonorrheal Earl of Rutland?'

'People who do not believe in the open line to the beyond,' she said. 'I don't think there's any use proceeding tonight,' she told her hostess, who moaned in distress:

'Oh, Mrs Allegramente.'

'You must flout the sceptic,' the academic said. 'You do not preach to the converted.'

'I don't like,' Enderby said, seeing in gloom a big cake like an Edwardian lady's hat swim from darkness to light and hearing coffee cups arattle, 'the assumption that I don't believe. I am, after all, a poet. There are more things, et cetera. Horatio,' he added to the lawyer. 'My stepmother,' he prepared to say.

'Perhaps you would prefer tea,' Mrs Schoenbaum said. Enderby heard a black whine from the darkness.

'No, no, no. I shall have tea when I get back to my room. Along with the Late Late Show.'

'The Late,' the academic, 'Late,' tasting every word, 'Show,' said. It was clear he had never heard of it. 'That is an amusing locution.'

'It's on television every night,' Enderby informed him. 'An ancient ah movie interspersed with commercials for cutprice ah discs.' He accepted a plate of white and bloody goo. The lawyer now began to disclose his madness. He said:

'Don't knock free enterprise. Free enterprise made this country what it is.'

'I'm not ah er knocking anything – '

'We don't need smartass, pardon me Laura, Europeans coming over here to knock American institootions. This next year we have our bicentennial.'

'As I am certainly well aware. My heartiest felicitations.'

'We don't need smartass sarcasm, pardon me Laura and Mrs Allegramente, from smartass knockers of American traditions. We celebrate two centuries of American knowhow. Also liberty of conscience and expression.'

'I most heartfeltly congratulate you.'

'Don't give us that. There's a tone of voice that grates on me, pardon me Laura. We're your one bastion against the communist takeover. So don't knock.'

'I certainly will not,' Enderby promised.

'There you are again,' the lawyer cried. 'It's the tone of voice.'

'I can't help my bloody tone of voice,' Enderby countered with truculence. 'I can't help being a bloody Englishman.'

'Who,' said Mrs Allegramente, 'is oppressing the Irish.'

'Ah, hell,' Enderby said. He would have said more, but at that moment the son Philip lurched in, probably stoned. He clearly reserved articulacy to his pianoplaying, for what he said, though long and partially structured, made no sense. But his mother understood him, for she said:

'I've no intention of marrying him, do you hear me, Philip? I've no intention of dishonouring your dear father's memory.' Enderby nodded at this apparent Hamlet situation. He did not however understand why this Philip, his gaunt stoned face encandled and dramatically shadowed, should look menacingly at him, Enderby. 'He takes you for someone else, Mr Elderly,' the mother explained. 'Tell him that you are not who he thinks you are.'

'I am not,' Enderby said loudly, 'who he thinks I am.' And then, in Duchess of Malfi tones, 'I am Enderby, not Elderly. I am Enderby the poet.'

This quietened the son down somewhat. He grabbed himself a hunk of the carved goo from the table centre and left noisily ingesting it. 'Good boy, good boy,' the academic said in relief.

'I think I'd better go now,' Enderby said, getting up.

'Oh no, oh no,' Mrs Schoenbaum cried in new distress. 'Mrs Allegramente has to convince you.'

'I'm already convinced,' Enderby said. 'There is a Happy House far far away.'

'*Not* far away,' Mrs Schoenbaum cried. 'Let's start, Mrs Allegramente.'

'Nothing will come through. Too much British scepticism around.'

'Let's have him telling us to get out of Northern Ireland,' Enderby suggested nastily.

'You see?' Mrs Allegramente said to Mrs Schoenbaum.

'Be good,' pleaded Mrs Schoenbaum. 'Promise to be good, Mr Elderly.' And she got up. Enderby muttered something about Mrs Allegramente's better being good, but this was not heard in the chairleg skirring. He followed his hostess and the others out. Their hostess led them to a small chamber off the hallway. The son was to be heard back at his piano, playing a single monodic line, one hand evidently busy with his goo. The black servant in the white coat nodded balefully at everybody, not specifically Enderby. He too seemed stoned. The small chamber was brilliantly lighted. There was a round table in the middle, four chairs of a dining order, a kind of throne for, presumed Enderby, Mrs Allegramente. 'No chicanery,' the academic said to Enderby. 'All above board. I have participated in previous sessions.'

'Is that so?' Enderby said. 'What is your ah specialization?'

'Pardon me?'

'You do what?'

'I run a course in theosophy. Saul Bellow is visiting us at the moment. He is deeply interested.'

'My kind of town.'

'Pardon me?'

'Be seated, all,' Mrs Schoenbaum invited. 'You will have the small lamp, Mrs Allegramente?' There was such a lamp on the table, a bulb of low wattage with a parchment shade. Enderby asked the theosophist in a low tone:

'Is that human skin?'

'Pardon me?' But Mrs Allegramente was already on her throne, breathing from the diaphragm. Look at the bloody man filling himself up with air. That had been said of AE, George Russell, prototheosophist, in sceptical Dublin. High on a throne like this, ready to speak of the maharishivantatattarara

64

or some such bloody thing. Mrs Schoenbaum, very eager, turned out the bright main light. Shadows, shadows and shadows. She put Enderby as far away as possible from Mrs Allegramente or whatever her bloody name was. She said:

'We all join hands.'

So Enderby had the dry bones of the academic on his left and the soft supermarket turkey breast of the paw of his hostess to the right.

'We may have to wait quite a while,' Mrs Schoenbaum whispered to Enderby after quite a while of waiting. Enderby nodded that he understood, quite a while, feeling, with a sensation of faint horripilation, that it was colder than it ought to be. Mrs Allegramente encouragingly groaned. Enderby realized he had neglected to micturate for several hours. His bladder, encouraged by the cold and not giving a damn whether or not it was astral, happily, like a dog, pawed its owner for walkies. Mrs Allegramente went: 'Oooooooh.' There was a sound in the room like the tearing of paper. Enderby did not like this. His bladder importuned. Mrs Allegramente said:

'Is there anybody there?'

There was a more irritable papertearing noise and then, after a minute or so, a hell of a knock on the wall behind Mrs Allegramente.

'One knock yes, two knocks no?'

There was another hell of a knock, though as it were structured like a monosyllable.

'Is that William Shakespeare?'

'I'm getting out of here,' Enderby said, hearing the wall banged in a sort of proud affirmation.

'Shhhh,' went panting Mrs Schoenbaum. Mrs Allegramente asked:

'Have you a message for anyone?'

There was no reply. 'Bloody nonsense,' Enderby muttered. And then he heard knocking on the underside of the table itself. There were four swift knocks, then a pause. There were six swift knocks and a longer pause. There were four swift knocks, then a pause. There were six swift knocks and a longer pause. There were four swift knocks, then a pause. There were six swift knocks and then silence. The damned table all the time tried to leap, but the spirit fist was not strong enough to raise it. 'Oh Jesus,' Enderby muttered. Mrs Allegramente could be heard breathing with decent, or non-spirit-raising, shallowness. 'No more?' Mrs Schoenbaum dared to ask. They all broke hands. Mrs Schoenbaum went to flood the room with decent brightness.

'It had the feel of a somewhat enigmatic message,' the academic said as they all rose. Enderby said:

'Pardon me. I'm afraid I have to – ' The lawyer grimly pointed.

Enderby found a small and overdainty lavatory off the hallway. He pounded his load out furiously. Enigmatic message his arse. His arse, thus invoked, spoke. 46 46 46. If that wasn't bible-amending Shakespeare, who the hell was it? Enderby did not like any of this one little bit. He wiped his penis on a handy face towel. Poor sod, proud of his contribution to the King James psalms. And now these New English Bible bastards had cheated him of his major triumph. Enderby pulled a lever which flushed the bowl, and, while it flushed still, left. Mrs Allegramente was waiting for him outside the door. She said:

'The message couldn't be clearer. It was QUIT ULSTER QUIT ULSTER QUIT ULSTER. Even you must have gotten the message.'

'Oh hell,' Enderby said, zipping up his not wholly zipped fly, 'it could have been KEEP ULSTER or KILL ULSTER or EGGS BOILED or BEER BLOATS or anything. But it was him all right. And you don't know why, do you, eh?' He wagged a finger at her. 'Leave him alone is my advice. Don't meddle. Good friend for Jesus' sake forbear, remember that.' Aaaaaargh. That was his stomach abetting. 'I'm getting out of here,' he said. And to Mrs Schoenbaum, who now hovered: 'I'd better telephone for a taxi.'

'Irving here,' Mrs Schoenbaum said, 'will drive you. It's on his way.' The lawyer beamed unexpectedly and said with overmuch cordiality:

'Well, sure, delighted.' This seemed to mean to Enderby that he would be dumped somewhere, having first been pistol-whipped, in the heart of flat Indiana. Enderby said:

'Thanks, but I don't want to cause trouble. A taxi will be fine.' He felt, obscurely, that he was involved in the causing of a deeper trouble than any there yet realized or, with such cultural equipment as they possessed, could ever realize.

5

The coming of April Elgar was harbingered by Enderby's coming onto the top sheet of his Holiday Inn bed. So, at least, he was to surmise. The lavish ejaculation was unwonted. It woke him at the useless hour of 4 a.m. Remarkable in man of your age, Enderby. He had not been dreaming of anything very specific. Later he was to see this as confirmation of the power of a woman he had not even seen and knew to be, which was pretty far away, in Miami, Florida. But she was having her bags packed for Terrebasse, Indiana, or rather for the Sheraton Hotel in Indianapolis, she being above Holiday Inns. And she was shooting out powerful erotic rays.

Holiday Inn bedrooms always had two beds, a thoughtful provision. Before getting into the so far untouched dry one, Enderby tugged the wet sheet free of its anchorage and then wondered what to do with it. Leave it to dry naturally and it would dry crinkled, announcing to the world of gossipy chambermaids the poverty of Enderby's sexual life. So he soaked the defiled patch in hot water and stretched it over a flat matt heat source. Then, naked as he was, he put on his glasses to examine himself with some care. There was no prevision in this: it was the marginal response to a marginally erotic situation, to wit an unpurposed seminal discharge. But there was also the matter of a long bathroom mirror. In Tangiers he had only a round shaving glass. Here you were cordially invited to look at yourself all over, no extra charge. He looked with interest at a naked man with spectacles on and no teeth in. This latter deficiency he fumblingly rectified. Better, but how much better?

There was fat there, but it was not slugwhite fat. He had got brown in Tangiers. Occasionally he climbed to the roof of La Belle Mer to sun himself. The sun was there and might as well be used. Bronzedness had a flattening effect: the Enderby that looked with interest and even faint approval out of the mirror was a less three-dimensional Enderby than the one he had occasionally seen before in the old days, that was to say, in other bathrooms. The encroaching baldness he did not approve. There were one or two members of the troupe who wore cowboy hats all the time, and one who wore a kind of Balaclava helmet of leather with earflaps. But they all had ample uncombed hair beneath. There was a shop near to the hotel with toupees in it. There was also, in Enderby's suitcase, a flat tout's cap with a peak that went back a long way and whose provenance was now very vague. The cook Arry he had known so long ago? Cut out a art shairped croutong with a art cootter. For piling on damson jelly as an accompaniment to joogged air. Enderby removed his spectacles and dug the cap out. Naked, he squinted at himself with the cap on. Anything went down all right in this mad America.

Enderby turned up at the theater next morning but one in the tout's cap and an overcoat of faded plum. He removed the overcoat to reveal blue linen trousers, an open yellow shirt with crimson foulard and a seagreen cardigan. He wore no spectacles. He could see enough, and some things he did not wish to see – the face of Toplady in full definition, for instance. He had to read a new scene to Toplady. There was no music in it really, so Silversmith did not have to be there. Before Will's sexual triumph following *Richard III* it had been decided to bring in brief homosexuality, espionage, violence and frightful death, in other words Christopher Marlowe. This was to scare Will and make him pack his and Hamnet's traps and ride back to Stratford, but then the Earl of Southampton was to appear and tell him not to. That would lead to Dark Lady and Southampton taking her from Will and her getting mixed up with the revolutionary party led by Essex. Toplady sat behind his desk apparently wondering at Enderby's new appearance while Enderby read aloud. First, though, Enderby sort of sang.

'There will we sit upon the rocks
And see the shepherds feed their flocks
By shallow rivers, to whose falls
Melodious birds sing madrigals.'

'Oh, good that, you must admit,' says Marlowe. 'Will Shakespeare here could not do as well.'

'Give me time.'

'Give us all time,' says Frizer.

'Amen,' says Skeres. 'But for some the time is ordained to be short.'

'Ah,' says Marlowe, 'very mystical and occult.'

'All may be clarified in time,' says Poley. 'Though not, of course, to everyone. You have worn a good cloak, Kit.'

'From the best tailor,' says Marlowe.

'I mean,' says Poley, 'the figurative cloak of your pretty songs about shepherds, and your loud brawling stageplays and your even louder atheism that the Privy Council chooses to ignore.'

'Ignore?' says Marlowe. 'I have been up before the Privy Council but recently. A matter of some blasphemous papers found in Tom Kyd's rooms. You know Tom Kyd, Will?'

'He wrote one good play,' says Will. '*The Spanish Tragedy*.'

The three men titter, and Will wonders why. Skeres says:

'That is not too apt. Much depends on what happens in the last scene. It is too soon to talk of the Spanish tragedy.'

'Come, come,' says Frizer, 'this is intended to be a merry meeting. Give me the lute and I will sing you a song, though not about passionate shepherds.' He takes the lute that Marlowe has been absently plucking and sings:

'As you came from the holy land of Walsingham,
Met you not my true love by the way as you came?'

'Ah,' says Poley, 'he knows the name Walsingham. It was, after all, his master's. His ears pricked like a dog's.'

'Sir Francis Walsingham,' says Skeres. 'Dead these two years, but once head of Her Majesty's Secret Service. He recruited you, Kit.'

'Sing him more,' says Poley, so Frizer sings:

69

'I sing of a spy, of a spy sing I,
That under the cloak of tobacco smoke
And drink and boys and blasphemous noise
Had sharp enough eyes for other spies.

'Meaning that he was, or is, a counter-spy, matching the Counter-Reformation.'

'Will,' says Marlowe, frightened, 'go and call in those men. The Privy Council men we told to wait in the garden.' Will tries to get up, quick enough on the uptake, but finds Skere's drawn sword at his chest. Skeres says:

'Nay, stay, we beg you, Mr Shakejelly. Play stuff, Kit,' he says to Marlowe, 'apt for the stage but not for real life.'

'I admit,' says Marlowe, 'real life has more surprises. I had no idea my three friends were creatures of King Philip of Spain.'

'You still have no idea, Kit,' says Frizer. 'You have no idea who we are working for, or, if thou wishest, *para quien nosotros estamos trabajando*. Why, we may also be working for Her Majesty's Secret Service, and that organization may deem it desirable to be rid of unreliability.'

'Look,' says Poley, his eyes stern on Will, 'this one here. Must he not too – ?'

'He is not quite a gentleman,' says Skeres. 'He carries no sword. He may freely report what he is about to see. The judgement of God on an atheistical roarer.' They all have their swords drawn. Will remains rigid in his seat. Frizer says:

'Draw your dagger, Kit. Let us have some little argument about the honour of a wench or who shall pay the reckoning.' He lunges at Marlowe. Marlowe draws his dagger. Frizer laughs, keeping at a sword's length's distance. He says:

'Ah, Mr Shakeshoes, are you not now in the great world? Did you not dream of all the glory of this London life when you wiped your snotty country nose on your sleeve?'

'Tell them, Will,' says Marlowe. 'Tell them what you have seen.'

'He may tell them,' says Poley. 'He shall corroborate all.' So all three now have their swords out, but they clatter them to the floor. 'Strike, Kit,' says Poley, 'strike, you passionate shepherd.' Marlowe holds his dagger indecisively. 'Now,' says

Poley. All three seize Marlowe's dagger hand and drive the dagger into his frontal lobes. Marlowe screams. Will is petrified.

'I still think,' says Skeres, 'we should dispatch this one too. A quarrel of drunken poets.'

'No, no,' says Frizer. 'It is a little man. Leave him.' And Will runs away.

Enderby looked up at the blur of Toplady, pleased. He could not tell from his look whether Toplady was pleased or not, but he took it that he was not, since he never was.

'Well,' Toplady began, and got no further. For his door flew open and in swam or sailed or flew April Elgar, saying:

'Hi.'

'Sweetie, marshmallow pie, angelcake' and so on went Toplady, half-rising and making a cold sketch of embracing her in hungry arms. Enderby not merely got up to give her his chair but retreated to the wall. 'This,' Toplady said with dramatic lack of enthusiasm, 'is er,' meaning Enderby.

'Hi.'

Enderby stood openmouthed underneath a poster for *Mother Courage*. He had never seen anything or body like this woman before. In Tangiers, true, he had presided, as owner of a perch of sunning ground windtrapped, over comely enough bodies and acceptable enough, if usually chronically dissatisfied, faces above them or, if they were lying down, at one end or other of them. These had been all white, meaning unwholesomely rich in greens and blues and carmines, and very pallid to begin with, earning slow increments of honey and ultimate toffee as the sun slowly chewed them. The women of darker hue he had been unable to judge of, since they showed only ankles under robes and kohled eyes over yashmaks. He had never really had standards for the assessing of black American beauty. This April Elgar was a revelation to his awed eyes, and would be even more so when he got his glasses on. She glowed in deep content with her Blue Mountain glow and exact sculpted line of feature. Quadroon? Octoroon? Blasphemous terms, obsolete musical instruments squeaking in accompaniment to a celestial choir. Denoting coldblooded blood apportionments apt only for damnable race laws. Doubloon was more like it: hot gold, also cool. The divine sinuous body was skirted in cinnamon, ensilked shins and ankles and feet shod frivolously on frail

71

plinths that were really artful engineering made Enderby groan with their frightful perfection. She had had pasted upon her a matching jumper of fairy chain metal. Her delicate breasts appeared unsupported. The hair, obligatorily raven, flowed a satin river, to whose blackness all blacks were chalk, scrawling their own reproach. She sat, well pleased with herself, by God, and no wonder, by Christ. She said, in a voice of cassia honey or an Elgarian string section:

'Has that fucking fag schlepped his ass here yet?'

'Don't be like that, Ape,' whined Toplady. 'You like Pete, you know you'll be great together.'

'What did you call her then?' cried Enderby in outrage. 'Did you call her what I think you called her?' She turned and looked Enderby up and down, as to appraise his fag properties, if any, and said:

'Ape he said, short for April, that's my name, honey.'

'Well, I won't have it,' Enderby cried. 'It's a bloody disgrace. To have so exquisite a name apocopized into the libellously simian. And you too with your bloody *Goats and Monkeys*,' he told Toplady loudly.

'Wow,' she said, 'you better write that down big so I can frame it and stick it on my wall. Good for the lip muscles. What's this,' she then said, 'about goats and monkeys?' She took a gold étui from her Bayeux tapestry bag. Enderby shook for his lighter and shook out a flame as she gave a white tube to her lips. She held his hand steady with long cool brown fingers. Toplady said:

'Our title. Right out of *Othello*. I knew you'd like it.'

'I get it. I'm the monkey and that screaming fag is the goat. Or is it the other way round? It's a lousy title. And in future you can quit calling me Ape.'

'Not dignified enough for its ah protagonist,' Enderby said. 'I think now that *Will* might be better. Will the name and the drive, sexual and social, you know, and even the final testament with the second best bed. With an exclamation point possibly. *Will!* Or two, if you like – *Will!!*'

'*Dark Lady*,' she said. She'd done some homework, then.

'With respect,' Enderby said, 'there's a play by Bernard Shaw called *The Dark Lady of the Sonnets*. Of course, she's not really dark in your exquisite and overwhelming manner.

Darkhaired only. Well, eyes too. My mistress' eyes are nothing like the sun. How about,' inspired, 'A Dark Lady's Will?'

'When do I start work?' she asked Toplady.

'Reading after lunch. I booked a table at the Escoffier. Silversmith will be back with some great songs day after tomorrow.'

'That fag,' she said. Enderby liked all this very much. But, of course, he, being British, had to be the final repository of faghood. 'Lousy British fag,' she would tell Toplady over luncheon, to which, Enderby did not have to be told, Enderby was not invited. She now ignored Enderby till she had finished her fag, which she had handled elegantly but on which she had drunk deep, discussing with hard impersonality the while various contractual rights which Toplady said could be clarified when the wife, Ms Grace Hope, of the screaming fag Oldfellow arrived with the screaming fag along with the other fag, screaming or not, Silversmith. Enderby was quick to wrest the exhausted lipsticked butt from her and grind it out in the concave plinth of some trophy, elongated humanoid, which stood on Toplady's desk. She stood and smoothed herself down laterally and said now to Enderby:

'What was that shit about exquisite apocalypse of the something something?'

'Not shit,' Enderby reproved. 'I don't wish to hear that word in your connection. It harms your beauty and elegance.'

'My my,' she said, with an oeillade meant to be comic. 'Okay, Gus, we go and all that sort of nonsense.'

'A fair warning,' stern Enderby said. She glided out and Toplady looked acidly on Enderby as he followed. Enderby lighted himself a Robert Burns cigar and coughed in a sort of delirium round the office. Her perfume, a complication of something expensively distilled in the town of Grasse and her own salt animal emanation, rode over the foul reek of nontobacco ingredients. Enderby went out, past the girl and women typists, and took the stairs down to the greenroom, where he gave himself lunch from the vending machine – yoghurt with boysenberries and coffee that went on wasting itself on the sugar-encrusted grill beneath. A dirty business. Later he went to the sort of classroom where, floor today unencumbered by the fag Silversmith, the troupe would assemble for the reading of Act One entire. He would have to read Will again. Soon he must surrender his lines to this screaming fag Oldfellow. It struck him with horror now that he must – The incongruity. God, they would laugh their heads off.

She was late, stardom's privilege. Toplady, being with her, also had to be late. Enderby filled in some of the waiting time by telling the lounging troupe about the kind of English they had, properly, to employ in their rôles. 'Remember,' he said, 'the *Mayflower*.'

'We ain't old enough, man,' said a black boy Enderby had not seen before. What the hell part was he to play? Henslowe? Sir Walter Raleigh?

'I mean, remember that the *Mayflower* brought over to America a kind of English very close to what Shakespeare and his ah contemporaries spoke. Do not attempt Sir John Gielgud accents, even if you know how. Speak the tongue of Boston, Massachusetts. It will be good enough.' He nodded kindly at them, who looked fuzzily, he being spectacleless, but unkindly back. Then April Elgar entered, followed by Toplady, and she looked at the men as if they were all fags, and at the others, which they were, frowsty frumpish sluts. She said, seated:

'Me.'

'I beg your pardon?' Enderby said.

'Me, me. Take it from where I come in, okay?'

'I,' Enderby apologetically said, 'have to read Will. Shakespeare, that is.'

'Okay. You wrote it. What page?' There was a fluttering of already soiled typescripts.

'Your name is Lucy,' Enderby said. 'There is a room with a pair of virginals in it.'

'A pair of who?'

'A musical instrument,' Enderby explained. 'Like a harpsichord. The Dark Lady plays it well. It says so in the Sonnets.'

'Well, this Dark Lady don't play nothing. Except a little stud poker.' Then she said very woodenly: 'Who are you, sir? Who sent you? You take a liberty, sir.'

'You summoned Richard the Third to your house,' Will Enderby said. 'You set your sights too low, madam. You should have asked for Richard the Third's creator.'

A pudgy ginger girl as duenna said, very woodenly: 'I knew he was not the man. Shall I have him thrown out, madam?'

Enderspeare said: 'The person of William Shakespeare is not handled by kitchen ruffians. I come as a gentleman to pay my respects to a lady. Get you gone, woman, and learn your place.'

'Very well, Marion. I will hear his message,' went April Elgar. 'Stay close and listen for my bell. Now, sir.'

'Your beauty,' Shakeserby said earnestly, 'deserves better than the homage of a mere player. You need a poet. A poet is what I am.'

'You are very forward, sir.'

'Come, none of this. I glory in your beauty. I have here a sonnet.'

'You have writ a sonnet? For me?'

'I have writ them for only one man – my near friend whom I love with all my heart, the Earl of Southampton.'

'So,' said April Elgar as herself, which was no different from as Lucy, speaking to Toplady, 'he's faggy.'

'Not at all,' said nonWill Enderby stoutly. 'He was omnifutuant. It was the way things were then.'

'Yeah, faggy.'

'Read,' commanded Toplady. Willerby read:

'But for one woman I have this:'

'So he takes out his shlong?'

'A sonnet. A sonnet. He takes out a sonnet. Shakespeare didn't write this sonnet. I did.' Enderby enWilled himself again. 'Hear, madam.

> 'All other beauty's light I lightly rate.
> My love is as my love is, for the dark.
> In night enthroned, I ask no better state
> Than thus to range, nor seek a guiding spark – '

'It is forward, to write of love so. You are very impertinent. I'll say he is.'

'I wrote this long ago to another lady, one I saw only in dreams. Now I see reality in your true and rich midnight darkness. I have always been seeking one such as you – goddess, genius, poetic pharos.'

'Poetic what?'

'Pharos, pharos. Greek for a lighthouse.'

'Okay, why can't he say lighthouse. Then it says that I play.'

'Where did you learn so delicate a touch? Surely not in your own country,' said Shakesby.

'I left my own country as a small child. I was torn away as a slave. I was brought up by a family in Bristol. It was a holy work to them to bring light to what they called the heathen. But then they freed me and made me into the lady you see, and when the father died he left me money.'

'Sing,' said Enderwill. 'A song in exchange for my sonnet.'

'Ah Jesus. You mean this?' And she minced out the words like a Moody and Sankey hymn:

> 'What doth it mean, to love?
> It is to plumb the seas and scale the skies.
> It is to wear the day away with sighs
> Or mount the moon above.
> Thus doth it mean, to love,
> So wouldst thou seek the truth of this to prove,
> And love?'

The entire troupe smirked at that. April Elgar gaped incredulous. 'It is,' Enderby stoutly said, 'in the Elizabethan manner. The sort of thing you'd sing to the virginals.'

'Sweetie,' she said, and then, in a kind of slave whine, 'ah doan want none of dem lil old virginals, whatever de shit dey are. Dey doan fit mah personality no way no how.'

'I've warned you before,' Enderby cried, 'about that sort of language. There's too much of this *shit*,' he told the whole troupe, 'going on. She there,' jerking his shoulder towards her, 'blasphemes against her exquisite beauty by bemerding her speech in that manner. For Christ's sake cut out the *shit* and let's be serious.' And he blazed his way back into the role, crying like a threat: 'You sing prettily, madam? Can you dance as well?'

'Some dances I can dance,' April Elgar said, first grinning and then not. 'The pavane – the galliard – '

'Canst,' Shenderspeare said, with a cunning change to the familiar mode, 'dance the Beginning of the World?'

'I know not such a dance.'

'I,' Spearesby said, 'will show thee.' And he beamed in embarrassment as pure Enderby.

'Well,' she said, in her proper person, 'we're waiting.'

76

'Oh, that. Well – he takes her in his arms and covers her with kisses. He imposes his will upon her, pun intended, he strips her of her taffeta elegance and carries her over to a gorgeous daybed. He untrusses himself and dances the dance called the Beginning of the World. A nice conceit,' he explained. 'The Elizabethans saw the sexual act in cosmic terms. It began with an image of creation and ended with death. To die meant to experience the ah orgasm.'

For the first time the assembled company responded to words of Enderby with something approaching attention and even respect. It evidently surprised some of the younger ones to learn that people who had been dead a thousand or a hundred years, same thing, knew about copulation and even had expressive figurative speech to decorate it in or with. 'Beginnin o the World,' the black lad said, drawing out *World* into something unglobular. 'I like that, man.' Before or after that night's Brecht nonsense some of them would be trying it out for the sake of the nomenclature. Baby, ah just died. Then a man in overalls entered to say that the Holiday Inn was on fire.

6

What had happened, so Enderby was to learn later, was that a disaffected busboy or bellhop, mandatorily stoned, had filled a familysize Coca-Cola bottle with gasoline siphoned from the hotel manager's car, glugged this inflammable out in the empty thirdfloor bedroom two doors away from Enderby's own and then enflamed it. He had then got the hell out with a cashbox containing something under a hundred dollars, there not being much cash around these days of credit cards. When Enderby got by taxi to the hotel he found a fire engine there, summoned from Indianapolis, with the firemen pumping not water but a grey chemical substance over all available surfaces. Not much of a fire, but the third floor had been evacuated. Enderby found his suitcase, fortunately closed, covered with grey dust and his decent clerical grey suit suited in a deeper grey. His tea mug and kettle were no longer around, but the rest of his stuff rested, along with other defiled luggage, by a pillar in the defiled foyer. He should by rights demand compensation for defilement but contented himself with getting the hell out, not paying his bill, and asking the taxi driver who had brought him hither and was staying to share in the excitement to take him and his defilements to the Sheraton Hotel in Indianapolis.

The driver insisted first on showing him the town he was to dwell in for a space, or it may have been a matter of his not knowing where the Sheraton Hotel was and hoping to find it by dint of cruising the entire city around. Central Park, Monument Place, radiating Massachusetts, Indiana, Virginia and Kentucky Avenues. State Capitol, Court House, Board of Trade building, Central College of Physicians and Surgeons, Blind and Deaf and Dumb Asylums. At length he said, with no hint of triumph, 'Well, here it is.' And there it was. Enderby expected sympathy from the reception clerk for his refugee condition and the state of his baggage but got none. But he was permitted to submit his suit for dry cleaning.

Lying on his bed, smoking a Robert Burns, he noted that he had been carrying all this while, and in spite of more immediate emotions and preoccupations, an inflated shlong, as she called it, and all because of her. Then he wondered about the fire and dismissed a superstitious supposition. Then he remembered that she was staying in this same hotel: he had heard a girl in the big open secretarial area of the theater's offices confirming her reservation on the telephone. Then he lusted for strong tea and raged in frustration. He would have to go out and resupply himself. He went down, overcoated though without his tout cap, and found a kettle and mug in a kind of hardware store off Kentucky Avenue and, in a supermarket entitled rather soberly EATGOOD, bought brown sugar lumps, canned milk and a box of two hundred tea sachets of unstated provenance, also a brand of toothglue he had not previously met called Champ. And then there was a new variety of stomach tablet named Whoosh. Rather exciting, really, all this consumerism. Fairly pleased, he took his purchases back to the hotel. In the lobby he saw Ms April Elgar. She was being silently admired, and no bloody wonder, by God. She was also flipping through mail that had arrived for her, frowning crossly at it. Enderby went straight up to her and said:

'Not much of a fire, really. But, as you see, I have been evacuated. I have the pleasure or honour of, both I suppose. As you observe.'

She did not at first seem to know who he was, a matter of his not wearing the tout cap, but his fag British accent presumably rang the bell of recognition that rang. 'Hi,' she said.

'A few essential purchases,' excusing the brown bags under his arm.

'I guess so,' distractedly. And then: 'You and me have to rap.'

'Rap?' Oh Christ, more spiritualist nonsense. 'I should be delighted to er.'

'Okay, the bar.' She swayed her way ahead to it. Enderby

removed his overcoat but found it necessary to hold it folded on his lap. The linen trousers were thin. An insincerely cheerful matron dressed like a whore took their orders: whisky sours for both.

'More sweet than sour,' Enderby remarked. 'Something of a misnomer.'

'You always talk like that?' she said. 'All these words.'

'Well,' Enderby said, 'the British have no real slang on the American pattern, I mean not one diffused throughout the entire social system, if you see what I mean. Also, I am a poet, Enderby the poet. Also, I live alone and speak little English these days. It's becoming, from the spoken angle, something of a foreign language for me.'

'What do you mean, live alone?'

'In Tangiers, with these three boys.'

'Jesus, so you're another of these screaming fags.'

'No, no, far from it, although you will, of course, naturally assume that all the British are fags. That's because your American fags tend to speak with a British accent. A bit illogical, really. Cart before the horse, sort of. I am unimpeachably heterosexual.' And, by atavistic instinct, he confirmed the testimony by slapping his crotch smartly. 'Too many fags around,' he added. 'Especially in the theatre.'

'You can say that again.'

'Too many fags a – '

'And dykes too. Listen. This is my show, right?'

'Well,' Enderby said with care, 'it's supposed to be Shakespeare's really. And let's get this straight about this er fag element in his life. He had an affair with the Earl of Southampton, no doubt about that, but it didn't express his true nature, which was passionately heterosexual. He had to climb through the pretence of ah faggishness. Not uncommon at that time. Their sexuality was so intense that it expressed itself in many forms. But in the sense that the Dark Lady is not only a woman but also a kind of destructive and creative goddess at one and the same time, and even perhaps a disease, well, yes, it is, to some extent your show.'

'So the opening number is me, a production number. I'll put the shake in Shakespeare, I'll put the spear in too. Establish,' she said, much in Enderby's manner, 'priorities.'

'Where did you get that from?' Enderby asked with some admiration. 'That's rather witty.'

'Just thought of it. Sharp as a pistol, brought up in Bristol. The white man's knavery sold me in slavery. Hey,' she hailed the serving matron. 'Two more of those.'

'Thou art,' Enderby said, 'as wise as thou art beautiful.'

'Oh, come on.'

'Quotation from. Titania says that to Bottom. But,' Enderby said with some urgency, 'the beauty is real enough, God knows. I say this with total objectivity. Your beauty is overwhelming, of a kind rarely seen. But this, of course, you must know.'

'Yah,' she said, 'I know it. My beauty is my bread,' she added with mock solemnity. 'Talent, too, baby, I got talent.'

'That,' Enderby said, 'I still have to see.'

'You better believe it. Right. That fag Silverass is on his way and you gotta have words to give him. Songs, baby. So I want you to steer your pinko ass into that elevator and get up to your room and start writing.'

'Gladly,' Enderby said. 'After dinner. I thought,' he thought for the first time, 'we might have dinner together.'

'That's nice, that's real nice. Like in old movies. Not tonight, baby, some other time.'

'You,' Enderby said, 'have already arranged to dine with some other ah guy. I see.'

'No, you don't see.' She sipped at her fresh whisky sour and Enderby at his. The tumescence was terrible. 'You see nothing. Ah has mah prahvit lahf.'

'At least,' Enderby said, 'you've stopped saying *shit* all the time. That's a word I've heard Americans use even at table. They don't take in the referent of the word. It's become just a neutral expletive.'

'Okay, no shit.' And then a great handsome man of her own colour, though much darker, bore down on their table. She rose in shrill ecstasy and they fondly embraced. Baby honeybunch and then an unintelligible duet in what Enderby took to be Black English. He drained his whisky sour unnoticed and unintroduced and stole off with his coat and packages. His shlong settled to neutrality. Black bitch and so on. Christ, jealousy, a dark wine long untasted. He hadn't come all this way to be jealous. He would leave it to her, bitch, to sign for the whisky sours.

But up in his room, strengthened by mahogany tea, he got out his yellow legal pad and started to scribble to her will. Lyrics, seeing her in a richly crimson silk farthingale belting them out, brown bosom fully exposed in the Tudor manner to proclaim, like the Queen herself, putative virginity. This vision was physically very painful. He had to cart the engorged shlong three times into the bathroom and, on a face towel mono-grammed with a fanciful S, fiercely discharge his heat. He saw himself fierce in the lighted mirror doing it and nodded fiercely at the fierce reflection. Then, less fierce, indeed encalmed, he went down to dinner and ordered a beefsteak and a half bottle of some ruby Californian muck, both restorative, indeed freshly inflaming. The waiter, a frail Viennese PhD immigrant, seemed to ask him what dressing he would take with his salad. No dressing because no salad. Green stuff was not good for you. April Elgar and her co-coloured fancy man were not there. Swiving like rattlesnakes some place. He, Enderby, willed himself not to care, finishing his french fries with his fingers, ordering apple pie with ice cream on it. Then he belched his way back up to make tea.

> The white man's knavery
> Sold me in slavery
> To an unsavoury
> Household.
> I slept in an attic all
> Foully rheumatical,
> Bedbugged and cobwebbed
> And mouseholed.
> I slaved like the slave I was,
> Ripe for the grave I was,
> But I was brave, I was
> Ready
> For my master's remorse and my
> Freedom of course and my
> Carriage and horse and my
> Monetary source
> Safe and steady.
> Now see me here in London,
> Ready for revenge –

> All England will be undone
> From Carlisle to Stonehenge
> On the dayyyyyyyy
> I get my wayyyyyy.

But here, by God, was corruption. You cease to celebrate the greatest poet in the world's history and ennoble nothing but lust of one kind or another. Goats and monkeys. Toplady was, after all, no fool.

> I'll screw some sex into Essex,
> I'll scourge Walter Raleigh's raw hide.
> I'll make Francis Drake
> Chase a duck on a lake
> And eat Francis Bacon fried.
> I'll inject the shakes into Shakespeare
> And stick in the spear as well,
> Wrench out Queen Bess's
> Carroty tresses
> And make her bald as a bell.
> Right under your gaze
> I'm going to raise
> Elizabethan hell.

Enderby groaned, but not now with lust, that foul fundamental whose harmonics were admiration, awe and even the most dangerous word in the language. He had been drawn into the celebration of America, not Shakespeare. What voice from the dead had condoned the travesty to come? Robert Greene, perhaps, putting on the tame tiger's hide in his cunning. One in the eye for Shakescene. Enderby got blearily off his bed (lyricizing was bloody hard work) and dug his contract out of the dusty suitcase. He should have read the small print before signing. Sold into slavery, by God. Suable if he reneged. Best to embrace one's enforced corruption. He started to write one more song before sleep.

> To be or not to be
> Smitten by you
> Bitten by you
> Teased as a ball of wool is teased by a kitten by you:
> That is the question
> Which harms my digestion

Marry, *à propos*. He swallowed six Whoosh tablets with chlorinated water and got ready for troubled slumber.

The next day Enderby left them all to it. Let the bastards get on with it. He tried to work in the hotel lounge, but perpetual sedative music got in the way of his rhythms. He went to see the bell bald manager about it, but the manager did not easily comprehend his complaint. Anaesthetization of the ear or something. Offwhite noise. He returned to his room to find the bed yet unmade, but he was used to unmade beds. He stuck the DO NOT DISTURB notice up outside and made himself more tea. Fed up, fucked up and far from home. He dragged Ben Jonson grumbling from his long sleep and made him sing:

> Ale and Anacreon,
> Beer and Boethius,
> Sack and Sophocles, these
> Please my heart
> More than the farting littleness,
> Borborygmic brittleness,
> Jokes and japes
> Of the apes and jackanapes
> One sees
> Courting the great
> At court, on estate –
> Fleas!

He foreheard the bemerding response to that and crumpled the yellow legal paper up. Yet he needed Ben Jonson to sneak in a few extra blank verse lines to make the revival of *Richard II* relevant to the Essex rebellion which immediately followed and thus have poor Will bemerded. Keep out of the great world, sirrah, stick to your word games. I, your Queen, tell you so. Lucky for you your head rolleth not like his, that runagate traitorous earl, on Tower Hill. Get you gone from my royal sight. Will was turning out to be a very bemerdable character.

Then he wrote lines to April Elgar:

> Edwardian brass, O enigmatic kingdom,
> Apostolic musicmaker, nobilmente
> Clashes the green roots, outyells returning swifts,
> Derides the cuckoocall. I cannot go on I

Cannot go on
Cannot
Enderby

He folded them into a Sheraton envelope, scrawled her name on, went downstairs overcoated, told the reception clerk to put it into her box. Surely surely. Then he went out to get drunk. He settled at length into a low bar behind the Board of Trade building. An old man whined to the bartender, who consoled him surely surely. Enderby ordered Scotch uniced and beer to pursue it. Workmen came in in hard hats. They heard Enderby's accent on his third ordering of the same again and derided his Britishry with what what and all that sort of rot jolly good eh old chap. They seemed to have watched a fair quantity of old films on television. Enderby grinned at them, unoffended. Then one man said that the Queen of England was a whore. Enderby grinned at him, unoffended. Then, Orpheus with his lute, he came out with:

'Four score and seven years ago our fathers brought forth on this continent a new nation, conceived in liberty, and dedicated to the proposition that all men are created equal. Now we are engaged in a great civil war, testing whether that nation, or any nation so conceived and so dedicated, can long endure. We are met on a great battlefield of that war – ' Then he took a drink. The workmen looked solemn, as in church: Lincoln's speech was a powerful cantrip. They bought Enderby the same again. He was told that it was only kidding about the Queen of England being a whore. He said: 'Her circumstances hardly allow it. Of course, your President Kennedy was a whoremaster or lecher, but that sort of thing is expected in a male leader. A double standard, you know.' Somebody put a dime or quarter into the jukebox hidden in the corner in deep shadow. It illuminated itself and thumped and twanged. Unformed male voices pitched high excreted nonsense with bad rhymes. Kennedy, he was told, slept with Marilyn Monroe. Now they were conveniently dead, both assassinated by the FBI, and were screwing away in heaven. No such place as heaven. It's got to be heaven if you're screwing Marilyn Monroe, you better believe it. Then the disc changed and Enderby heard a known voice:

'Give the world a kiss
Although it rates a kick
Get in double quick
And give the world a kiss'

'Ah God,' he said. There, said somebody, is another one that screws. All dinges screw, they got no morality. She's here right now in Indianapolis, screwing. Screw a dog, screw a beer bottle, bottom end. 'Oh God,' moaned Enderby.

'There may be roars
But there are roses
A fiddle and a flute
There may be wars
But underneath your nose is
Juicy fruit still unpolluted'

Juicy fruit, I'll say. Give the world a fuck, I'll say. Enderby had to get out. You tell the Queen of England from me, fella, she ain't no whore. Enderby was surprised to find it dark without, street lamps on, hail spinning lazily down. He had been there longer than he thought. He wove his way back to the Sheraton. He carried his key in his pocket, always forgot the number. He made several stabs at the wrong door, somebody yelled, muffled, 'Who's there?', then found his own, 360. That number meant something, he couldn't for the moment think what. He fell inside, doffed and threw at the television set his overcoat, then fell on the bed.

He was awakened by knocking. He got up with considerable difficulty and groaned his way to the bathroom door. It was not at that that the knocking was proceeding. He opened another door and blinked painfully. She, paper in hand, dispossession notice. She wore scarlet tailored slacks and matching jumper, heavy beaten bronze earrings, scarfed montage of European cathedrals about her throat. Enderby's heart thumped from drink. He bowed her shakily in. She sat down on the one chair with arms and looked at him. He said:

'I heard you singing. In some low place. Not you personally, of course. I must take something. Heartburn. If you'll excuse me.' He went to the bathroom for Whoosh and water. He came back with a foul headache. He sat on the edge of the bed. 'That in your hand,' he said. 'I see what it is now. Doesn't make much sense. Nominal fantasy. Had to go out. Drank a little. My apologies.'

'What gives with you?' she said. 'I've never met any dude quite like you.'

'Double agony,' Enderby said. 'I adore Shakespeare. I adore you. Somebody has to be betrayed. You'll swallow him. You're swallowing me. Old as I am. Ugly. Unworthy. You try that on for size,' he said with bitter jocosity.

'You mean you want to get laid?'

'That's right,' cried Enderby, head cracking, 'bring it down to animality. Things aren't as easy as that. Shakespeare didn't want just to get laid, as you put it. She was stitched into his senses, made his soul drunk. He cured himself, but only through his art. He had to lose his only son first. Oh yes, sex came into it, with all its connotations, universal, cosmic, yin and yang, ultimate sex. You don't get over it by screwing, as those men said.'

'Which men said?'

'The men in the pub, bar. They said the Queen of England was a whore. You can't complain if they said the same about you. Bloody animality. Then we come to the most dangerous word in the language, and you know what it is. A declaration of faith with little hope and not much bloody charity. Why aren't you with that bloody man you were with last night?'

'What? Who? Oh, him. That was Ben Jonson, my brother, and don't call him bloody. He plays piano with Mitch Frobisher's combo. Ah, the greeneyed dingus. And so you get paralytic.' Not a just word, he considered, looking down at his tremor. He said:

'Jonson with an aitch, I suppose. Without would be going too far. Although there's an aitch in Westminster Abbey. And where does the Elgar come in?'

'He was a British composer. I always liked that what I used to call when I was a kid Pompous Circus Dance of his.'

'He wrote a bloody sight more than that,' Enderby said. 'Edwardian hubris and neurosis, an incredible combination. And I suppose the April is really June.'

'Not far out. May Johnson, brought up Baptist. If they want to fantasize over the April Elgar image, okay, let them. That's what it's there for, I guess.'

87

'Funny,' Enderby said, 'girls are called after spring, only men after summer. Augustus, I was thinking of. But of course that's the cart before the horse again. Forgive me.'

'Like that thing in Kant, I guess. Noumenon and phenomenon. May Johnson is the dingus an sich.'

Enderby gaped. But, of course, everybody in this country got educated at the State U, a kind of superior high school. Then they forgot their bit of education in order to make money. Very sound, really. And then they could paralyse their interlocutors with Kant when they didn't expect it. 'I'm parched,' he said. 'I have to make very strong tea. Will you join me? But I only have this one mug. I'll buy another tomorrow in case you. You can use this one first and I can swill it after.'

'Real English genlmn. But it's dinnertime. Wipe that white stuff off of your mouth and drink three glasses of water. Then I take you up on us having dinner together, okay?'

'I couldn't eat a thing.'

'Then watch you lil friend eat.'

The three glasses of water prescribed renewed the heartburn ferociously, but a couple of powerful martinis at table put him right: the headache merely hovered over like the awareness of a decorated ceiling. He felt he could tackle red meat. He looked with tolerant disapproval at April Elgar's cottage cheese and salad with thousand islands dressing. His tumescence did its best to find its aetiology in the Aprilian and Elgarian and leave May Johnson alone. How bloody beautiful she was, each functional eating gesture a shorter lyric. Men at other tables kept sneaking glances of envy at him. No one could say: that ugly old bastard is her father. And sick desire at her. Their wives ignored him and knifed her with bitter hate. Enderby monologuized, awaiting his red meat. 'Salads dry up my saliva. Green things have something unnatural about them. The most dangerous word in the language, as I said. Onanism is a logical safeguard, you know, a device of protection of the deeper emotion. Nobody wants to lust after people: images are what are required. Though love is a bloody nuisance. Helen's beauty in a brow of Egypt. Funny he should say that disparagingly. He felt differently when he got to Cleopatra.'

April Elgar picked on that along with a forkful of salad. She said: 'Right. Cleopatra. Think of Cleopatra and you won't go far wrong. Stick an asp on my left tit if you like at the end, but it's me they got to remember. A blaze of gold, you see that?'

'Don't use that word,' Enderby groaned.

'Which one?'

'That one.'

'Tit? Sorry, old boy, old boy. Bosom. Breast. Knocker.'

'Oh my God.'

'We'll beat the bastards, you and me. May sheow, eold felleow.'

7

Enderby sat in one of the many toilets of the Peter Brook Theater reading a paperback volume of what were known as Science Fiction Stories. He sat long partly because of a costiveness that seven Gringe tablets had so far done nothing to ease. Perhaps, after all, salads were healthful. Too much protein and starch. For breakfast he had eaten pancakes and maple syrup and sausages on the side. He had brought his own steaming mug of tea down with him, an eccentricity now accepted by the Sheraton. Must do something about diet. Must not reject little paper cup of coleslaw issued with lunchtime sandwich. Spinach munched from can like marine character in old cartoons with ridiculously overdeveloped forearms. He sat long sequestered also partly because there was such a hell of a row proceeding at rehearsal. Clash of characters, egos really. That fag Pete Oldfellow and the divine April Elgar were creating, with claws distended and genuine hurled spittle, more compelling drama than any dramaturge could contrive. God was still, after all, so Enderby ungrudgingly conceded, the best of the dramatic poets, though shapeless and uneconomical. A bit like Charles Dickens. God was good on the physical and emotional sides and a great one for hate. He generously spilled his own hate into his dearest creation. That's why you had to have Jesus Christ, who unrealistically overstressed the love part. But God hated him too and sponged him out one Friday afternoon. The play now enacted on the dimlit stage was God's play, though God had to leave it to people to provide an ending.

Enderby read about people travelling to imaginary galaxies. God, if he would only grow arms and learn how to write, could do this sort of thing much better. The monsters on the planetoid Anatrakia were very anthropomorphically conceived. There seemed to be a lot of this sort of thing around, alternative universes ten a penny, and the young actor who had lent him this volume for a quiet lavatorial read boasted of possessing over four hundred science fiction paperbacks. Ought to have volumes of Shakespeare, really, Sophocles, Racine, Ben Jonson, others, but didn't. Didn't take his paid art seriously. Dick Corcoran from Manticore, near Toronto, Ontario, playing Essex and understudying the fag Oldfellow, who was making a very peevish job of Shakespeare.

Enderby read a story about the inhabitants of Garagogoki, the capital city of Berkibark on the planet Urkurk, who gave birth to little machines of no apparent purpose but produced babies in flesh factories. If the parents, or purlerguts as they were called (a term roughly meaning beneficiaries), did not discover the purpose of their machine within four orgs, a measurement of time relating to the periodic explosion of a renewable sun called Maha, the machine, which grew steadily to a monstrous size, Molochlike devoured them. The hero and heroine of the story, named Arg and Gogogoch respectively, tried to smash their machine at birth, but this resulted only in fissiparous replication of the monster. Enderby was deeply absorbed in this implausible narrative when a voice above his head said:

'Mr Enderby is urgently wanted on the telephone.'

No escape. There were loudspeakers everywhere. He discounted the allegation of urgency and wiped himself, alas, drily. There was nothing urgent for him, at least not on the telephone. He had managed to get through to Tangiers yesterday and, except for the explosion of the frying machine in the kitchen and a fire quickly doused, everything seemed to be all right there. *Muy bien. Adios.* Enderby took his time getting to the telephone in the main office and there heard a woman's voice say to his earhole:

'Mr Elderly? Laura Schoenbaum.'

'We must really, you know, get this business of the name properly sorted out. I am Enderby. Enderby the poet.'

'Oh, so glad you're there. Mrs Allegramente didn't want me

to but I'm doing it just the same. Nobody else could say what it meant, but I'm sure you can.'

'Another tabletapping session, eh? A lot of nonsense. Somebody pretending to be William Shakespeare, eh? There's a lot of malice going on back there, ought to have something better to do with their time, eternity that is. What was – '

'Well, yes, it was the Bard himself from the Happy House and he just made the same sound three times. Through Mrs Allegramente's mouth of course, which was wide open, she was in a trance.'

'What was this sound?'

'Well, it sounds kind of silly – kha, kha, kha, just like that. And then a pause, and then the same again. And then another pause, and then the – '

'Kha, kha, kha?' asked Enderby. Girls looked up from their typing. 'Or was it more ha, ha, ha, though with a very strong aspiration?'

'You could say that, I guess, yes.'

'Hha, hha, hha, then,' Enderby said. 'Fairly clear, I should think. There's a sonnet beginning with the line "The expense of spirit in a waste of shame", and it warns about the dangers of lust. The sin of animality. Then comes the line that begins "Had, having and in quest to have", and there's no doubt that he's mocking the noise of lustful panting. Dog and bitch on heat. Men too. Women also perhaps.' Typing had not been resumed. 'So he's reminding somebody not to get caught up in the toils of unconsidering sensuality. Hha, hha, hha, eh? Of course, it may not be Shakespeare at all. Just somebody who's read him.'

'There was nobody there it would apply to, Mr Elderly.'

'You can never be sure,' Enderby said darkly. 'Hha, hha, hha.'

'Well, thank you, I hope everything's going all right there.'

'Everything's going just fine,' Enderby said, as he heard the screams of April Elgar and Pete Oldfellow approaching the secretarial area and Toplady's office. 'Hha, hha, hha,' he said in valediction. And he put down the handset.

God, how bloody beautiful she was in a rage. Her raging elongated sunset of a rehearsal suit, a onepiece jersey jumpthing, turned her into a flame with teeth. Enderby's heart melted. Behind her, glum and nailbiting, was Toplady. They were going to have it all out in a kind of privacy. Oldfellow whined, but he had neither her vocabulary, suprasegmental tropes of remote jungle origin, nor her numinosity. He was a man of about Enderby's size with a nose that would not get in the way in kissing sequences, mean blue eyes and a pouting mouthful of porcelain crowns. With him was his wife, Ms Grace Hope, a thin woman in a ginger trouser suit and an extravagant fair wig. To her Enderby abruptly addressed himself, saying:

'A question of money. There are two hotels requesting nay demanding payment. My own resources are not ah unlimited. I invoke the terms of my contract.'

'Later,' Ms Grace Hope said. 'At the moment the show itself is in jeopardy.'

'Not through any fault of mine,' Enderby said. 'I've done everything required. Totally accommodating.'

'A smidgen too accommodating,' Oldfellow said. 'My part's been slashed to fucking ribbons.' And his head with its mean blue eyes tocked to April Elgar and ticked back to Enderby. Enderby said:

'I'll thank you not to use that word in ah her presence. Nor, for that matter, in the presence of ah her.' Meaning Ms Grace Hope, his wife. 'Questions of propriety.'

'Don't give me that kind of shit,' Oldfellow said. 'I know what's been going on around here.'

'In,' Toplady said with weary bitterness, his nailgnawed right thumb showing in where.

'What precisely,' asked Enderby of Oldfellow, 'are you suggesting?'

'Oh, for Christ's sake,' Toplady said, entering his office first.

'Myself also?' Enderby asked.

'Yeah, yourself also.'

'Why,' Enderby asked Toplady, when they were seated, 'are you called Angus?'

'I don't see what the shit that's got to do with anything.'

'What I mean is, the Scottish blood, if any, is not made manifest in any – Well, a certain directness of utterance, though usually coarse and improper, an apparent passion for whisky: that bottle on your desk is now empty but was full yesterday – '

'I get this for lagniappe,' Toplady told everybody.

'They were going to call him Agnes,' April Elgar said, 'but when they got a closer look – '

'Stop it, stop it, stop it,' Oldfellow screamed.

'Right,' Ms Grace Hope said, a very hardfaced woman. 'We keep our tempers, right? And we talk about the script. A musical's changed while it's in flight, we know that, but there've been too many changes behind Pete's back with no consultation. He's the star, right? He plays William Shakespeare, right? He gets the script and he says okay, lousily written but that can be put right later, and then when he gets here – '

'Who,' Enderby said, 'says that it's lousily written?'

'You may know Shakespeare,' Oldfellow said, 'but you don't know the theater. There's a difference.'

'You don't know the *theater*, either,' Enderby said. 'You're what is known as a film star.'

'Oh, for Christ's sake,' Ms Grace Hope said, a sudden winter sun shaft firing a faint lanugo Enderby had not before noticed, so that her face seemed to bristle, 'let's stick to the point. This is supposed to be a musical about Shakespeare.'

'Which it is,' Toplady said. 'It's also about the Dark Lady.'

'It's about the Dark Lady,' April Elgar said very sweetly. 'It's also about Shakespeare.'

'You see?' Ms Grace Hope told a poster.

'Well,' Enderby mumbled, 'the concept was bound to change. The talents of Miss ah Elgar here have to be employed. The emphasis is on the power of certain ah dark forces on the life of the poet. I admit there was no such emphasis before. The emphasis now seems to me to be a just one.'

'Thanks, kid,' April Elgar said.

'Practicalities,' Ms Grace Hope said. 'We want certain things restored that got cut out behind our backs.'

'This plurality,' Enderby said. 'Do you speak as ah Mr Oldfellow's wife or as his agent or as ah what?'

'I,' she told Enderby, 'am taking this show to Broadway. There's money being put into this show on certain strict understandings.'

'I assumed,' Enderby said, 'that Mrs ah Schoenbaum – '

'That applies here. It doesn't apply when the show takes off from this theater.'

'What she means,' April Elgar said, 'is that she's producing a musical to show that the great overpaid Pete Oldfellow is more than just a pretty face.'

'Listen who's talking about overpaid,' Oldfellow hotly said. 'I do this fucking thing for peanuts and she – '

'I will not,' Enderby cried, 'have this continual debasement of language.'

'Ah Jesus,' Toplady went.

'All that's needed,' Ms Grace Hope said, 'is cooperation, right?'

'Okay, tell that fag of a husband of yours to cooperate, okay?'

'I will not be called a fag by this black bitch.'

'Ah, I knew we'd get that sooner or later. Okay, maybe this black bitch better schlepp her black ass off home.'

'He didn't mean that,' Enderby said. 'And you didn't mean that about his being a fag.'

'Didn't I just, brother.'

'She calls everybody a fag,' Enderby explained. 'She calls me a fag too, but I don't object.'

'Baby,' April Elgar said, 'you may be an uptight ofay milktoast limey bastard, but you ain't no fag.'

'Thank you,' Enderby said gravely. Pete Oldfellow said in heat:

'She's got him by the balls, she's made him pussydrunk, she eats him for dinner.' Toplady cried:

'We've got less than one month before opening. This can't go on.'

'Well, try a smaller size, baby,' April Elgar said.

'I'll say one thing,' Enderby suddenly said with weight. 'This thing is not entirely in our hands. There are too many messages coming through. Not very coherent perhaps, but we're being warned, I think, not to play ducks and drakes with the dead. I'm no more superstitious than the next person, but there have been various signs.' They all looked at him. Ms Grace Hope said:

'What do you mean – signs?'

'Mrs Schoenbaum has these seances, superstitious nonsense, of course, but there seems to be somebody out there, watching. A fire at the Holiday Inn. My fryer back in Tangiers exploded.'

'You're crazy,' Oldfellow said without conviction.

95

' "Good friend," ' Enderby said, ' "for Jesus' sake forbear – " ' '

'Jesus,' went Toplady anticlimactically.

'A thought, that's all. We're trying to celebrate, in a popular and rather ah American form, altogether appropriate considering the double nature of the celebration, the human side of a great poet. That human side must not be traduced. The dead seem to have their own way of responding to the law of libel. If anybody's going to be made to suffer, it's going to be me. A fellow poet. Letting the side down. You,' he said sternly to Oldfellow, 'had better watch out. You're acting Shakespeare like a kind of cowboy. And with what I take to be a Milwaukee accent. Shakespeare's not going to like that.'

'You're crazy, that's for sure,' Oldfellow said, now with conviction. 'And I come from Cedar Rapids, Iowa.'

'Listen,' Toplady hissed at Enderby, 'I'm director, okay? And I'll decide who does what and how. You just give what you're asked for, okay? That's laid down in your contract.'

'It's also laid down in my contract that I get some money.'

'Give him some money, for Christ's sake,' Toplady said to Ms Grace Hope. Ms Grace Hope at once gave him some money out of a big canvas bag covered with widowed letters of the alphabet in various typefaces. Enderby thanked her courteously. 'Okay,' Toplady said, 'next call's at two. Entire company. Act One.'

'That fag,' April Elgar, 'that plays piano. I want him out on his fat ass.'

'Mike Silversmith always has him,' Toplady patiently explained. 'Mike Silversmith needs him.'

'I don't need him, brother. And I don't have him.'

'Silversmith,' Enderby pronounced, 'is musically analphabetic. His sense of prosody is rudimentary. This fag, Coppola I gather his name is, is at the moment necessary. He can notate music.'

'Who,' Toplady said viciously, 'is running this show?'

Enderby bowed to everybody and then took his urgent engorgement and the image of April Elgar off to another toilet. Then, having finished the implausible story about the planet Urkurk, he went off to have a beef sandwich with coleslaw, which latter he ate.

That afternoon, from a lonely seat in the dark auditorium, he watched Act One unroll. The Induction was back in. Then Elizabethan London was primarily April Elgar and a dumpy woman choreographer. Oldfellow gawped at London, gumchewing kid as dumb Hamnet holding his dad's paw, and gave it slow hayseed (Cedar Rapids, he had said) greeting. He had prerecorded his songs, cheating but permitted in a star who had never sung before, and to the thumping of a live piano by the bald but hairy Coppola opened and shut a soundless gob. April Elgar did not warble Enderby's little Elizabethan pastiche about love; instead she belted out gamier words, though still by him, Enderby:

> 'Love, you say love, you say love?
> All you're talking about
> Is fleshly philandering,
> Goosing and gandering,
> Peacock and peahen stalking about,
> Squawking about
> Love,
> He-goat, she-goat, mare and stallion,
> Blowsy trull, poxy rapscallion.
> You'd better know that my golden galleon
> Is not for your climbing aboard
> Of'

And so on. And it was not right. She was shaking her divine black ass to it. She was black America, which was better than Cedar Rapids, but she was not Elizabethan London. Nor, God help him, were his own rhythms. And another thing: what right had he, Enderby, to assume that Shakespeare had fallen for a genuine negress (inadmissible term nowadays, he had been told)? A dark lady was not necessarily a black lady. A chill fell on Enderby. He had been corrupted in advance, he had *wanted* a black lady, and nobody had questioned his assumption. Another thing: the dialogue was being steadily corrupted to modern American colloquial. Pete Oldfellow now said, in his Shakespeare persona: 'Okay, then, let's forget it.' Enderby yelled:

'No!'

Toplady, who sat in the centre aisle at a table with a light trained on his script and notes, looked round from over black-framed reading glasses at the source of the agonized cry, then he counteryelled:

'Out!'

'Are you talking to me?' a quieter Enderby said, while the cast looked down.

'Yeah, talking to you. And what I said was.'

'I know what you said. Am I to sit here and hear that bloody traduction and make no bloody protest? I said no and I mean bloody no. And if you haven't the sense of historical propriety to say bloody no too then you're a.'

'You want to be *thrown* out? You're barred from rehearsals, get that? When I want you I'll let you know, right? Now get your ass out of here.'

'Bugger you,' Enderby said doubtfully and getting up. 'The whole thing's a bloody travesty. I'm getting out. I'm also going home. Bugger the contract.' And he climbed panting up the deeply raked aisle. When he got outside into the dusking concourse or whatever they called it he breathed deeply and angrily. Also impotently. He had no return ticket nor money for one. He had, in the toilet, counted Ms Grace Hope's meagre handout. He had neither publisher nor literary agent in New York. He had no source of money to get him to what he called home. He lighted himself a White Owl, better than Robert Burns though not much, he had been recommended to try Muriel but he had once known a girl called Muriel, and he looked through the great window at the dusking carpark. Snow spun on blacktops and, tautomorphically, white tops. Gonna be a white Christmas, they said. He turned to snort smoke at the double door whence he had exited and puff disdain at what lay within. Then the doors opened to show April Elgar running on long legs out. Ah God, that damnable beauty, crystalline and coral concern, body like flame, arms like lesser flames towards him. Then she had him embraced, and he, White Owl awkward in gripe, had to embrace back, then throwing White Owl to hoot out disregarded smoke on oatmeal carpeting. Recover it later.

'Honey, honey,' she said, 'we'll beat the bastards, you'll see.' Then she raised her lips (only a little way necessary) and kissed, with surely histrionic though instinctually histrionic sincerity, him, Enderby. Who dithered. Who trembled kneewise. Who groaned. Who said with little breath:

'You shouldn't. You know. Changes world. Forces me to. Avowals. Most dangerous word in the.'

'I'm with you, baby. Screaming fags. Just thought I'd let you, you know, like know. Ow.' That was Enderby's embrace unwillingly pressing the air out of her. But a sturdy tumescence more appropriate to her image than to her pressed reality thrust them, in the first phase of its arc, apart like some instrument, a truncheon say, of moral order. One of her sharp metal heels transfixed Enderby's White Owl and it ceased, though not for that reason, to smoke. Enderby, seeing it, said:

'Ought to. Give it up. No breath, you see. Don't make me. Avowals.'

'That bastard Topass insulted you, kid, and I've come to take you back in there. You got your rights. He's gonna pologize.'

'I don't,' Enderby said, volume of SF at groin, 'want his bloody apologies. I wouldn't go in there again if I was dragged. I'd be on the next plane if I had the money. I'll lock myself into that bloody cell with the electric typewriter, obscene thing purring at you all the time, and I'll do what has to be done. Then I'll get paid and I'll bugger off. Forgive my bad language.'

'You coming back in there with me.'

'No, I'm not. And there's another thing. The whole damned enterprise is becoming farcical. Quite apart from Oldfellow's stupidity and incompetence. I mean, there's no sense of the past in it. I mean, what with jazzing things up and you, forgive me, wagging your divine ah buttocks.'

'Divine buttocks. I got to remember that. I'm singing the songs, right, saying the words, right, acting this Dark Lady, right? It's that fag Oldass that's fucking it up, right?'

Enderby sighed profoundly. 'It's as if there's no sense of the past here in America.'

'Well, who wants the past? Like the cigarette commercial says, we've come a loooong way, baby. This past you talking about is a bad bad time. You ask my mother. You coming back in there?'

'No,' Enderby said. 'I need tea.'

8

So, in the second act, Essex and Southampton come to see Will and tell him to organize a revival of *Richard II*, signal of rebellion. I cannot, my lords, it will be taken as treasonous. Is not the sale of the book of the play banned by the Privy Council? Thou hast thy responsibilities, Will. Did I not give thee a thousand pounds that thou mightest purchase a player's share in thy bedraggled and mouthing acting company? (True. Enderby had inserted that truth in the first act.) Aye, my lord, and did you not steal from me her I was besotted with to become your own mistress? Come, Will, thou knowest that she but used thee as a rung on a ladder of advancement. She is now our Boadicea. Oh, what bloody nonsense. A song for the rebels:

> Who'll fight for Essex,
> Our uncrowned king?
> From Anglia to Wessex
> Let affirmation ring.

Oh no oh no no no. He, Enderby, was encircled by discouragement, and when, as from her with the divine black ass and the other attributes of magnetism, he was granted encouragement it was in the direction of the further bemerding of poor Will, more, the whole of his spacious age. So the rebellion failed and the dissident earls were confronted by Toplady's silly mistress, who had to be thought of as Gloriana. You, sir, I confine to jail since you were but a foolish follower of this ingrate that knew not what he did. Mayhap my successor, a man of royal lineage whose nomination must be kept secret for fear of such as my almost late lord here, will release you at his royal pleasure. But this, this, this foul viper and toad of the commonweal, this flouter, this sneerer, this minor satan in trunk hose and foolish smirk, shall to Tower Hill and his condign end. Aye, his head shall roll with the smirk wiped off by death's tersive napkin and no more shall be heard of him. Where now is this black and evil tigress in a woman's hide that I hear of? Let her be brought before me that I may look on her and consider best of whether she shall live or die. So April Elgar swings her divine black farthingaled ass into the royal presence, and one in decaying ginger pallor looks on the fabled gold of Afric. Oh Jesus Christ, this never happened and it never could have happened.

Enderby nevertheless heard in his head all too clearly, dealt by an evil muse, a conflatrix of the spirits of bemerded Will's poetaster enemies, chirpy words in the tones of Mistress Lucy Negro, played by April Elgar. Madam, queen you may be, but it is of a blanched and bleached kingdom unblessed by the sun, a nearly quondam queendom leprous, decayed, weakly tyrannical. Know you not where the future lies? Look westward, sister/ from this derelict/ island, a blister/ soon to be pricked. I speak for the future, madam, Cleopatran New Rome, I speak of black power,/ that's what we'll get;/ although I lack power,/ I'll get it yet.

The response to all this of the spirit of Shakespeare was not reported from Mrs Schoenbaum's residence, since she was spending a week or so in Miami, but small and as it were distracted punishments dogged Enderby's residence at the Sheraton. He got himself stuck in the elevator, between floors too; he fell heavily in the bath, a proof that, anyway, baths were dangerous; plugging in his kettle to make tea, he somehow managed to fuse all the lights of that floor; he slipped on a patch of ice in the forecourt of the hotel; he was served a decayed shirred egg. He was glad to get back to the Holiday Inn in Terrebasse. Shakespeare's spirit, having many preoccupations, probably mainly to do with the price of formerly Shakespeare land in Stratford's environs, would not find him there again, not being concerned to listen in to Ms Grace Hope telling him, Enderby, that the budget for a writer had to be kept low, stars costing so much, the Holiday Inn was where he had been put in the first place and that was where he should stay. Question of taxi fares also from Indianapolis to the theater. In Terrebasse he could slither on the brief ice between place of work and of repose. Well, it was just as well. Corruption because of proximity of, most dangerous word in language. Oldfellow too much around in bar and dining room too, when Ms Grace Hope had returned to California, betraying faggishness, a genuine attribute, not just conventional smear from April Elgar, by pawing his understudy, primarily Essex, Dick Corcoran the SF man. Get the bloody job finished, get air fare, get home.

'You not been around much,' she said to him one day when they met by chance, indeed coming simultaneously out of neighbouring toilet doors in the Peter Brook Theater. Enderby eyed her bitterly, trying to look like disguised Rosalind in some ridiculous black trendy production of *As You Like It*, that was to say in peaked corduroy cap and patched boilersuit, but breathing very quintessence of elegance and glamour. He also looked guiltily on her, since he had decided to get rid of her at the end of the first act. He could not go on with this ahistorical nonsense. Christ, they were dealing with real and documented situations. Toplady and she could do what the hell they wished, but he would not be a party to their falsifyings. 'Where,' she said, 'you go for Thanksgiving?'

'Thanksgiving?' he said. 'Oh, yes. Of course, that's why they served turkey and pumpkin pie, ridiculous washy stuff. I'd nothing,' he said, suddenly sorry for himself, 'to be thankful for, really. Besides, they were a hell of a long time achieving a reasonable harvest. The Pilgrim Fathers, that is. Good theologians but bad farmers. No, I just stayed where I was.'

'Where you going for Christmas?'

'Same thing, I suppose. Turkey and. Perhaps they don't serve pumpkin pie at Christmas.'

'Christmas,' she said, 'you're coming home with me.'

Enderby took that in very slowly. 'Home?' he said.

'Not my apartment in New York. Home where my momma is. And the kids. In Chapel Hill, North Carolina.'

'Kids? Which kids?'

'*My* kids. Bobby and Nelson. Five and seven. My momma looks after them.'

'And who,' dithered Enderby, 'is their father?'

'Their daddy done go away,' she slavesingsonged. 'I tell him to get the hell out. He was prime meatjuice, baby, but he done hit the bottle and was a real no good mean nigger. Now he's in a black stud agency for white women some place.'

'In what,' Enderby asked, 'capacity do I? That is to say.'

'Momma,' she said, 'don't hold with poets and showbiz people and all that crap. She's a gooood woman. Reads the bible all day. You got to come to momma's house that I bought for her out of my sinful showbiz success as an Englishman spreading the word of the Lord, kind of a smalltown Billy Graham, dig, I worked all this out in mah lil what ah calls mah mahnd, you got to be called Reverend. You'll be okay, momma cooks real good.'

Enderby had read in some magazine of soulfood, strange name, as though the soul resided in the lowliest of animal organs, intestines, hog's bellylinings, spleens. Perhaps it did, black wisdom. Also mustard greens.

'And,' she said, 'she makes tea good and strong in a quart brown pot, ladling it in by the shovel. She drinks it all day when the kids are at school, reading her bible. You better bone up on your bible, Reverend, don't want to be caught out.'

Enderby warmed at once to the quart brown pot. 'That goes with the name Johnson,' he said. 'Dr Samuel Johnson, great tea drinker. Boswell said he must have had exceptionally strong nerves.'

'How did you know that,' she asked, surprised, in a straight, or American straight, voice, 'about Boswell? My great grand-pappy was called Boswell Johnson.'

'Some learned and facetious slaveowner,' Enderby said, catching with no pleasure an image of elephanthided men called Cudge whining under Simon Legree whips in the cottonfields, what time old massa in the parlour read with mild interest a great record of the conversation of the English Enlightenment. And then: 'Alas, I have no money. I can't afford the fare.'

'I pay, baby. Ah is a rich lil gal.'

'Well, then, yes, thank you, it's a great honour and you're very very generous.' Then he began to weep, he did not know why. The voice of Toplady sounded over loudspeakers, its very tones giving him a partial reason why, calling the company together. 'Sorry,' Enderby sniffed, 'ridiculous, I know. Emotional lability. Creative tension, something. Again thank you.'

She laid on him hands intended for comfort but provocative of a ferocious glandular gear change and said: 'Something's going on in there, I know. Life's not easy, kid. We'll talk again, okay.' And she darted off, showing a cunningly placed patch, affluent mockery of the Third World to which her colour entitled her to belong, but Abe Fourscore had changed all that, on her divine posterior. Enderby returned to his little room and switched on the electric typewriter, which sang gently to him of the need to work and not waste current. He relented somewhat (there was always this danger, adjacent toilet doors or a jaunty 'Hi' in the greenroom) and did not wipe her wholly out of Act Two, no confrontation of queens but mention of her part as evil genius of uprising, and then she was to languish in some jail or other or be thrown onto the ragheaps of Clerkenwell, no more be heard of Mistress Lucy Negro except as pocked whore. But then.

Then there was *Hamlet*, Will as ghost misnaming prince as Hamnet, sick for many reasons (death of son and end of Shakespeare line; his lordly friend Southampton in prison; the loss of a rare mistress, brightness falls from the air or hair) and sent off to Stratford to be made whole. And in marital embraces with ginger Anne (it had been decided, and no bad idea, to combine the parts of queen and Mistress Shakespeare) he dreams of Afric gold, Egypt being in Africa. And so Cleopatra. But who was he, Enderby, to adapt a great tragedy to the limited talents, New World phonemes and intonations and slangy lapses, cecity towards the past, Pyrrhonism and so on of this weak cry of players? A straight blank verse Cleopatra, and she could not do it. Dumbshow to music (not Silversmith's, better to drag in some genuine musician from Indiana University, a Moog man who, forced to write tonalities wholly atmospheric, would produce the diluted romanticism that was his true, if suppressed, idiom?)? Enderby lighted a White Owl. Let Rome in Tiber melt, and the wide arch/ Of the rang'd empire fall! The world well lost for love, and did the world include art and, for that matter, William Shakespeare?

> Let's have one other gaudy night,
> Let's have one other bawdy night
> And fright the white owls away.
> Come, captains, drink beneath the stars
> Until the wine peeps through your scars,
> Drink till the dawning of the day!

For some reason that needed a black voice, altogether male and fully ballsed, but it had to be the fag Oldfellow transformed in vision to a Will with a chest like twin kettledrums. And for her?

God knew, she was Cleopatrician enough as they boarded the plane for Chicago, she in plain moulded emerald dress with seagreen cloak that had flared in the wind as they left the taxi, he in cap and old overcoat, blinking without glasses. At Chicago they got on an aircraft bound for Raleigh, named for the father of smoking. Smoking, she said:

'Now, honey, you can talk.'

'What about?'

'You know what about, kid.'

Enderby sighed like furnace. 'You mustn't,' he said, 'consider me to be a sexless recluse advancing into grey middle age. I live alone after a brief failed marriage. Unconsummated, indeed. She was a woman of great chic and skill and ambition, and she wanted to be married to a poet. Then she became well known as a manager of pop groups and similar abominations.'

She looked at him wideeyed, new angle on him. 'Who?'

'A certain Vesta Bainbridge who became a certain Vesta Wittgenstein.'

'Oh Jesus, her I knew. She wanted to manage me one time. She was a bitch, one hundred per cent and no discount.'

'Well, there you are then. The muse was very angry about it and went away. I couldn't write. I attempted suicide. Then I was rehabilitated, as they put it. Then she came back.'

'Who came back? La Wittgenstein?'

'No, the muse.' Enderby looked very gravely at the smoking goddess beside him, a meanly framed vista of American bad weather beyond her. 'Personification, if you like. Writing poetry isn't like adding up figures. There's a force outside that gets inside and starts dictating. Easier to call it the muse. Her, I mean. She can be very jealous. She's gone for good now, I think. So much and no more is granted to a poet. I've published my *Collected Poems*, to no applause. What I do in that bloody theatre or theater is nothing. Pure craft. Not so pure either. I hope I'm not boring you.'

'No, honey. You just keep straight on.'

'My feelings towards ah your divine self, then. With a woman a man has to effect a dichotomy. You know the word?'

'Oh, come on.'

'Sorry, you keep assuming this Topsy act, the slangy front to the world, the virtues of deprivation and so on. What I mean is. Well, it was you who mentioned the noumenon and the phenomenon aspect of things. I take your image to bed with me and devour it growling. Need, you know, the filling up of the wells. Disgusting but ineluctable. A private indeed privy matter. But behind that is you, and yet not behind that, because your body is no mask. And if I say love – ' The aircraft responded to that dangerous word by meeting clear air turbulence. ' – I mean, what the hell can you do with love except cleanse yourself of it by debasing the image to a lust object? I mean, what do I say, I, an ugly ageing man whose skin was never washed in the sun's glory, running a beach restaurant in Morocco, all all alone? Marry me, prove that marriage can work, companionship and all the rest of it, let the love derived from total knowledge rub off onto the image and make it no longer an object of concupiscence, do I say that? Of course not. I suppose,' he said heavily, 'I wish to invoke a special relationship, impossible of course.'

'Yeah yeah yeah. Quite a speech.'

'And what,' Enderby asked, 'do you do about love? If I may ask.'

'I tried it. Now I have my career. Not simple then, is it? You don't just want to get laid.'

'Getting laid,' he said, 'solves no problems. Love is a bloody nuisance.' CAT agreed. 'And we have the business of this damned musical play to make matters worse. Because you're not Cleopatra. Divine, beautiful, heartstopping, a miracle of flesh and bone and air and fire but not Cleopatra. You see that?'

'Yeah, baby,' sighing like smaller furnace, 'I know. I'm me. But I'm being paid to be me. Me singing songs and – what was the expression you used? Wagging my divine buttocks, yeah.'

'And that fag Oldfellow as you rightly call him is not Shakespeare or Antony either. And I'm stuck in this thing, mired in it, and I can't get out. Look, that damned thing's on fire.'

'Port engine? Yeah, it does that sometimes. How's about my songs?'

'It's still on fire. No, it's gone out now. No, it's started again. Saw me getting on this plane, giving me warning. Leave his dust alone. It's gone out now. No, it's not. Yes, it has.'

'Songs.'

'One song. You can be Cleopatra in a kind of dumbshow, Will's vision. Then he gets drunk with Ben Jonson – '

'You're crazy.'

'Not your brother, the other one. He dies of a sweating fit, and he sees you for one last time in his delirium. Love of his life. Inspiration. The future. Nature. Sex. Libido. The dark unconscious.' Enderby kept his eyes warily on that port engine. It did not reflare. 'The trouble is the words. The trouble is that that bastard fag Silversmith doesn't understand prosody. The trouble is going to be the music. One song. Summing it all up.'

'To be or not to be,' she said. 'Pure what's the word ontology.' Enderby looked at her with some awe. 'To be or not to be, what is it you want of me, what am I to you except the one thing true that fades, evades, lives in the shades or a world unborn shorn of reality, no actuality, a dream, a gleam of gold unmined you'll never find.' Enderby wished now heartily to embrace her: what she was improvising complete with tune was, God knew, terrible enough but it would get the whole damn burden cleared off his shoulders, the godless task finished. But they now had to fasten seatbelts and prepare for landing. A lot of cold flat green. 'I did some Creative Writing at Chapel Hill,' she explained. When they were standing in the aisle to get out, following and followed by blacks and rednecks, none of any great beauty or distinction, he did attempt a tentative embrace. She was a slim girl, not much to get hold of. 'Hey, hey,' she said.

107

She drove them both expertly in a hired Avis Studebaker or something down what seemed to be dirt roads and then a highway towards the town of Chapel Hill, where also was the first of the United States state universities. Enderby did not know what to expect of her momma's house. No log cabin, certainly, redolent of chitterlings. It turned out to be a nice little detached dwelling in pink brick with a flower garden, just behind a hotel called the Carolina Inn. There was an aged black hoeing.

'Hi, Uncle Joe.'

He dropped his hoe in a clump of dead morning glories or something and went 'Wha howya hawa wah haha yeah' or something, chuckling his grey black head off. Then he came to the car to start taking bags out of the boot, trunk they said here, making to Enderby a similar speech, not however chuckling. 'Hi ah,' Enderby offered, straightening his tie, which, he knew, was royal blue with gold spots. And then he followed her up steps and into a nice little hallway smelling of aerosol magnolias. And then.

Well, he lay awake that night of Christmas Eve digesting his welcome, expressed best in many mugs of mahogany tea, also a homecooked meatloaf. Her momma a welcoming woman with grey curls, old, she the divine one a product of ageing loins, in a royal blue sack of a gown with gold spots, her body gross with the enforced farinacity of long deprivation. Lemme looka you Reverend, with sharp old eyes blurred by a milky meniscus. You faaaaar from home for de birt o de Lord Jesus, and so on. An upright piano and on it photographs of family large, dispersed, done bad to by whites, Ben and little May grinning at making grade, the father long dead in bogey accident on railroad. The kids, Bobby and Nelson, televisiongawpers like other kids, showing no enthusiasm at sight of festive square packages from Indianapolis. You take dem walkin Reverend while me and ma daughter has lil talk. So Enderby had to walk the main street of Chapel Hill, empty of college students because the vacation was on, with a little black kid in either hand. This was not something he had foreseen. The kids rolled eyes of suspicion up at him but also demanded Cokes and ice cream sodas. They also demanded to be taken to one of the town's two cinemas, where a Swedish travesty of *Fanny Hill* was being shown. No kids allowed, he told them. He walked them back very wearily and at first could not find the house, nor could they, but at length saw the gardener wrenching up plantains and growling some ancient song of bondage. He and the kids had a brief colloquy that Enderby could not understand, and then the three of them went in. April Elgar had turned into May Johnson, in sloppy dressing gown and old mules, hair disarrayed and a daughterly whine. Enderby one of the family then.

He lay in the bedroom that had been intended, it seemed, for Ben the son, who had however Christmas engagements but telephoned from somewhere to his mother, who said you just do dat son and we be thinkin of you and lovin you just de same. After the meatloaf and collard greens and a Sara Lea creature, strong tea but no alcohol, Mrs Johnson opened up her bible, put on spectacles and looked over the top of them at Enderby. Enderby felt fear: he was going to be tested. But all she said was what your favourite psalm Reverend, and he was able to answer Psalm 46 and even quote some of it at her, so that she nodded and checked and said dat right Reverend. And then she said: what you goana preach about tomorrow Reverend and that made him spill his tea on his tie. She had him there in the corner of the combined living and dining room at the cleared table, while May Johnson had her arms about the two kids on the biscuit-coloured settee, watching Bing Crosby and Fred Astaire in *Holiday Inn*. 'The meaning of the Nativity,' Enderby said, and she nodded and quoted about de census to be taken ob all de world in de time ob Caesar Augustus.

Well, he lay there. Mrs Johnson lay in the room next to his, her daughter in the room beyond, and the two kids on a two-tiered bunk in the room beyond that. This was neither the time nor the place to entertain lewd thoughts about April Elgar, so he lay there partly illumined by a sodium street lamp working out tomorrow's sermon. Of course, this had been inevitable and he, or that blasted divine girl there, ought to have foreseen it. Distinguished visiting inevitably Baptist preacher all the way from England. It was not to give a sermon to Baptist blacks that he had come all the way from Morocco. He ought really to try to convert them to his own brand of apostate Catholicism, but perhaps Christmas was hardly a discreet season for that. Soon, a Holiday Inn face towel stuffed inside the crotch of his faded striped pyjamas in case of accidents, he slept. He slept remarkably well, and was wakened in southern winter sunlight by a small black boy bashing him on the shoulder and offering him a mug, no inscription on it, of very strong hot tea. The other black boy was with him, and then May Johnson herself came in in dressing gown and worn mules to wish him a merry Christmas and even to hand him a small gaudily wrapped gift. She also kissed him on the lips, her lips being warm from sleep and also greaseless, while the two kids looked solemnly on. Fortunately he had slept with his teeth in. He said, unwrapping:

'Oh my God, you shouldn't, I didn't get anything for. Oh my God, oh just what I wanted.' It was not really, being a miniature calculator to be worn on the wrist with a dusky screen that showed time playing the game of numerical transformation, squarish figures becoming other figures with the minimum of dim-lit metamorphosis. The day, and all the days to follow till the end of the world, were presented to Enderby as a linear process, not the fall–rise cycle of the poet. As for calculating, what had he to calculate? He looked at her, sitting on the bed edge, with humble gratitude, saying: 'It was a problem of. Well, you see, I had to pay the hotel bill.'

'You gave me a poem,' she said.

He could not now very well upbraid her for getting him into this Reverend situation. He offered his tea mug to her but she shook her head. Enderby slurped. The voice of Mrs Johnson below called them to breakfast. The kids, jostling each other for precedence, ran. She remained seated, lovely though not, the deglamorized daughter, mythical. 'Strange,' Enderby said. 'Here we both are, in a clinal situation so to speak, a bed context I mean, the Greek word means to lean or repose I suppose, hence bed, hence clinic by the way, and this has nothing to do with my feverish imaginings. Domestic, I mean. I weep at the impossibility of it all.'

'Momma has breakfast ready. Eggs. Ham. Hominy grits.'

'I'll write you a proper poem,' Enderby said. 'You'll see. I weep at the.'

'Yeah, yeah, impossibility of it all. Say, there's a good title for a song, Cole Porterish. The impossibility of it all, the sheer futility of it all. You must work on that.'

'Even bad art,' Enderby solemnly said, half-empty mug in paws, 'is made out of elemental cries for help.' But she had gone.

Mrs Johnson sang crackily a song about the itty bitty baby born in Baithlaihaim as she served breakfast. Here was he, Enderby the all too white man, Bradcaster pink mitigated by Tangerine bronze, at home, dusky Morocco a mere station in its direction, in a black household. He could see himself for ever here, drinking ever stronger tea and reading the Book of Deuteronomy with Mrs Johnson, cracking the kids' woolly heads when they were fretful, waiting for the daughter-Female Friend-goddess-impossible she to be deglamorized on a flying visit. After breakfast of two fried eggs and ham and a sort of white porridge (get dem greeerts down, dey'll do you gud), he shaved, dressed in Christmas clerical (all metaphors in time become reality) grey, then trembled. God knew what he could do about this bloody sermon. Leave it to chance, muse, Holy Ghost? Cynicism. Compoundedly dangerous American visit. Surely the God of the black Baptists could not be less vindictive than dead Will?

They were driven by May Johnson down the main boulevard of Chapel Hill, Enderby at back flanked by kids. Both ladies were demurely hatted and gloved. They arrived at a whiteboard building of simple pseudocolonial charm between a Howard Johnson restaurant that looked much more like a church, spire and all, and a garage where hammering artisans defied Christmas. The chapel had its own carpark, and this was already full of Plymouths and Oldsmobiles. There were a lot of women waiting to go in, all blackly radiant in the mild sun, and black respectable men in decent suits. Big treble event this, evidently: Christmas, big singing star back in hometown, foreign Reverend: Mrs Johnson had clearly been busy on the telephone. A genuine or right Reverend, named on the outside board as Dr R. F. Grigson, greeted Enderby with warm black hands and secular gusto. A big man took Enderby on one side and handed him his card: Condor Life. You travellin a lot, Reverend, your dearest and nearest in need of first class protection, we have lil talk after service. Then they went into a plain place of worship with a dais, a lectern, and an electronic organ. The worshippers, gleamingly teethed and boldly coloured, were stained glass enough.

It was not at all like the Catholic masses of Enderby's youth, dyspeptic Maynooth leprechauns peevish about last week's collections, or the anaemic evensongs of his brief curative Anglicanism, with fine if archaic Jacobean prose apologetically delivered by cricketing rectors and very well-made hymns bleated by conservativeclubcakebaking etiolated housewives with herb gardens. They went in a lot for extravagant joy here, also a healthy concern with sin. They cried yeah, that right and we hearin you. May Johnson, as he ought to have expected, sang what was called a gospel song to a jazzy accompaniment from a young buck whose grin mimicked his two electronic manuals, while the congregation clapped in rhythm:

> And when I get to heaven where I belong
> It gonna be Christmas all eternity long.

They smiled on him with encouragement and expectation when he was called upon. He stifflegged it to the lectern and surveyed them all sickly, fine bright open godly black sods as they were, no, not sods, decent people really. May Johnson expected the best from him, he could see that. Not let her down. He had given, when in the army, lectures on the British Way and Purpose, now very remote entities and never easily definable even then. He had delivered a disastrous speech when receiving the Goodby gold medal for poetry, which, along with the meagre cheque that went with it, he had at once given back. He had always found it difficult to be insincere and that perhaps was why he had not got on in the world. He was worried now about the danger of sincerity breaking in. He was not worried about either articulacy or audibility. They would hear him all right. He said:

'My name is Enderby.' They all smiled at the quaintness of his accent. 'Enderby the poet,' he unwisely continued. They did not now all smile. 'So they call me sometimes in my own country, because I have endeavoured to praise the good of life and deplore its evil, and do other things as well, in the medium of verse. There is nothing wrong with being a poet, so long as one's poetry is not obscene or Godless or ill composed. King David, as you all know from your psalms, was a poet, and King Solomon, he er – ' – he was not sure whether son or father, like a character in *Ulysses* – 'was also a poet, as you know from the Song of Songs that is his. A poet can be a witness for the divine posterior, that is to say truth, and he can thus be a martyr, which means witness in Greek.' The Reverend Grigson went amen at that. 'Now tomorrow is the feastday of St Stephen, who was battered to death with stones because he was a Christian, and you know who ordered the battering – Saul, who later had a sort of epileptic fit on the road to Damascus and was changed into St Paul.' To some in the congregation, including Mrs Johnson, this seemed to be news. Enderby had already lost his connection. Poets. Martyrs. 'William Shakespeare, a great martyr or witness for the truth, put himself into Psalm 46 – look it up after your Christmas dinner or even before – forty-sixth word from the beginning, forty-sixth word from the end, if you omit the flourish *Selah*.' Some of the older and ignorant, who presumably believed that the King James version was the direct word of God, no nonsense about having to go through the Hebrew first, showed wideeyed shock. 'Do not be afraid of poets,' Enderby cried bitterly, 'since they are often God's instruments, though they can also be the devil's as well, though not usually at the same time if it can be avoided.' Then: 'Martyrs, I said, and I say again martyrs. Your people have been martyrs, witnesses to the devilry and Godlessness of racial oppression. You think of the white man as the enemy, but I ask you to remember that white men have suffered, if you can accept the Jews as white, women too. My own people suffered in England in the times of the Godless Tudors, a sort of gingerhaired people from the principality of Wales, not of the race of the fish, mammal really, that swallowed Jonah, if you can believe that, a whale's throat being somewhat narrow.' They all looked at him in wonder, no cries of dat right and I hearin ya. 'My family stuck to God's truth as taught by the Church of Rome, and, by Christ, we suffered for it. Later, of course,' he added speedily, 'we became Baptist, another true faith battered by the forces of oppression. Oppression,' he then cried, 'intolerance, hatred – ah, by God, do we know them? By God we do, and will go on knowing them. Today, as some of you will know, we celebrate the birth of Jesus Christ in a filthy stable. He was on the side of intolerance, saying I come to bring not peace but a sword, and on the side of hatred, as of the Pharisees and of even your own father and mother if they got in the way of the truth and the light. Christians have been oppressors throughout the history of the faith, as you know, for it was at least nominal Christians who oppressed your people during the dark days of slavery. Christians oppressing Jews as well as blacks as well as Muslims, for the most part teetotal pederastic people, and of course the other way round, although neither Jews nor blacks have had much opportunity to be oppressive, except in Israel and Africa. Still, everything comes to those that wait. Some call slavery and oppression modes of cultural transmission, meaning that if you had not been enslaved and oppressed you would still be worshipping stocks and stones and sucking jujus in the heart of darkness, well, not quite, most of you coming from West Africa, an explanation of your natural artistry, don't bother to try to learn Swahili, that is an East Coast *lingua franca*. Therefore I ask you to move forward,' he said, 'forward to an age in which none of these things will happen, except in the Godless media, of which the damnable stage is one, and try to get on with the job, whatever it happens to be, insurance or singing or bongo drumming, and let us try to make a little money for our children and our children's children and, if the hideous future which has not yet come about but, by heaven, will come about will permit it, even our children's children's children, yea, unto seventy times seven. Not that I personally, so far as I know, I was briefly stationed in Catania in World War Two, have children of any colour whatsoever. Today is the feast of the holiest of all the children and, by God, let us not forget it. *In nomine Patris et Filii et Spiritus Sancti*,' making the sign of the cross, '*Amen*.' Then he got down.

9

They were sitting together on the flight back up north, so she had been retransformed into April Elgar, and very lovely and mythical with it. Her hair, newly straightened, was all ink and health. She was else fresh Blue Mountain coffee mixed with the morning's milk, scarlet too, dress and liprouge and finger-nails and, as Enderby knew though scarlet leather hid them, toenails as well.

'That's what she said,' she said, 'when you weren't there, in the john or some place.'

'In the er yes,' Enderby corroborated. 'Never ask me to be insincere again. God won't attack, anyway. He could see through the confusion. A great one for sorting out chaos. In London on a hoarding I saw DEVLIN THE BIG NAME IN DEMOLITION. I misread that Devlin, naturally. It's the other up in Indiana we have to watch. Shakespeare, that is.'

'It's not Indiaaaaahna, it's Indianna, like in bananna.'

'Banahna,' Enderby corrected. 'That thing with jam and sliced bananas and custard your ah momma made was very good, took me back to my infancy. The turkey was good too, very crisp on the outside. But strong tea is her real, appropriate when you come to think of it, forte. She said I ought to stay on and help look after the kids and have some real good home cooking. She seemed to think I was not very well. A conse-quence of.'

'They're charitable people,' she said, 'and don't you forget it. My momma told everybody you been working too hard and got the word of the Lord all balled up. That's charity.'

'*Caritas*,' Enderby said. 'Well, she's welcome to come to

Tangiers. Kids as well. Do them good, they can learn Moghrabi Arabic and be black Muslims or something. No, they can't, being Baptist, I see that. You too,' he then said. 'You'll knock them ah cold.' He then saw her very clearly lying naked in the sun and felt his flesh respond terribly. But she wouldn't lie in the sun, brown enough already. He spread *Time* magazine over his crotch. She said:

'That's in Africa some place, right?'

'North. The kingdom of Morocco. Not what they call Black Africa. This unitary concept you get over here from some of those woolhaired louts is a load of ah nonsense. Africa's very big, you know. So big that nobody can swallow it. They huddle into tribes in self-protection from it, you know. Anyway, we're all exiles. You and I, anyway. As for colour, that's only like furniture. A green chair or an orange one, it's for putting your fundament on. If white's no good it's because it has the wrong connotations. Leprosy, slugs, and all the rest of it. It's not real white anyway. If you think I like being white you're wrong. I see myself white writhing over your divine brownness. An abomination. I beg your pardon. Shouldn't have ah externalized that vision. Better off as we are,' he added vaguely.

'How do you mean – as we are?'

'I love you,' Enderby said boldly. 'I shall love you till the day I die. There,' he added unnecessarily, 'I've said it. Demand nothing. Totally disinterested. Perhaps,' he superadded, 'I can start writing poems again. Love poems. From a distance. Me white in Africa, you black here. Not really black, of course. A damnable politicoracial abstraction. There,' he finished.

She sighed out cigarette smoke. 'Brother,' she then said, 'you sure are one large pain in the ass.'

'Unfair. Disinterested. Ask nothing. If you wish, I apologize for that ah declaration. We're coming into Chicago now, my kind of town, sorry, that's back in Tangiers. Then back on the job, forget what I said. Partners in crime only. It *is* a bloody crime too. The things we're doing to Shakespeare. Then I pack your divine image among my dirty shirts and go. Love poems.'

'Pain,' she varied, as they prepared to get out, 'in the divine fundament.'

'What God showed to Moses,' Enderby said, following her

down the aisle. 'I've often wondered why. God with a bottom. Some very profound significance.'

When they had marched a mile or so, to the accompaniment of ubiquitous Vivaldi, nice change from pop, pop of its day when you came to think of it, to the area whence the aircraft for Indianapolis took off, Enderby at once sat down and chewed a couple of Pepts. Silversmith was there, with two other men. 'Hi,' he offered. He effected laconic introductions. 'Len Bodiman, orchestrator. Pip Wesel, MD.' Bodiman carried a heavy canvas bag which presumably contained what would be called the score. His glasses, in heavy black mourning frames, were too big for him, and he kept them on by variously grimacing. He was a big soft man in a kind of Churchillian sirensuit. Enderby said:

'What kind of orchestra? Shawms, recorders, viols da gamba, sackbuts? Authentic, I mean?' It was this Pip Wesel who replied. Enderby assumed that Silversmith's rude terming of him as Mentally Deficient was either a joke or a tribute to his creative madness in whatever field he wandered, scenic artistry perhaps, but the young man, who was chihuahua-hairless, was full of uncoordinated gestures and he now bleated several times. He said:

'We've been hearing about you. Mike here said that's what you'd say. You want madrigals too? Hey nonny nonny and all that shit?'

Enderby felt his neck getting thicker. 'Don't,' he threatened, 'use that word in the presence of this lady here.' April Elgar was standing somewhat apart, and Enderby saw himself, with bitter regret, as physically not very disjunct from these three ugly leerers. White and unbalanced, paunchy and full of tics. He pulled in his own belly since he could not push in theirs. He had a vision of April Elgar writhing on a bed with a black man of comparable beauty. He nodded with desperate regret and satisfaction. April Elgar said:

'Save your breath, kid. He's crammed with that er commodity.' She had learned something from him, Enderby, then. Wesel said:

'Okay okay, colleagues, right? Working together, right? Peace and love and all that shit, right?'

'There you go again,' Enderby said. 'And what precisely is your ah role in this enterprise?'

'MD,' Wesel said.

'That's frank, or perhaps facetious, but what is it precisely that you do?'

'He wags the stick,' Bodiman said. 'He's the stickwagger.' And then, to April Elgar, 'You got rhythm yet, Ape?'

'Don't,' Enderby began, 'call – '

'One of the big black fallacies,' Bodiman continued. 'Rhythm as the inborn inheritance of the jungle.'

'I got more rhythm in my ass,' April Elgar said unwisely, 'than you got in your whole fat sluggy ofay corpse, brother. I can see we going to get along just fine.'

'Shakespeare at work,' Enderby pronounced. 'Sowing dissension. It's the curse he prophesied. Moving his bones.' But nobody listened. They had been told through a loudspeaker to get on the aircraft, but Bodiman found the opportunity to say:

'In your ass, right,' and she:

'What's that supposed to mean?'

'He's not referring,' Wesel said, 'to your singing, if that's what it's called.' And then he skipped ahead, bleating. If Enderby had had the money, he would have limped back through the crowds and Vivaldi to the international segment of O'Hare, there to purchase a homeward ticket and get, as they said here, the hell out. But he was chained. On the aircraft, next to an April Elgar who brooded and drank whisky sours in excess, by some dispensation, of the number allowed by the paternalistic airline, he gloomily regarded his new digital watch, faintly fascinated by the onward march of the square figures which turned one into the other with insolent ease, a kind of numerical paranomasia. Then he switched the instrument to a calculator and added up large sums.

He was adding up even larger sums on his bed later that day, having eaten hamburger steak with fried eggs, drunk lager that tasted of onions and water, taken Pepts and Windkill, then sadly onanized. He should rightly have done so to the stimulus of April Elgar's present, but it was not aromatic of her as a shoe or stocking would have been. The present was really an unwilled invitation to accept a very dull future in which one second was the same as another, as symbolized by the minimal metamorphosis from number to number, in which the achievement of a minute and later an hour was, so muted was the change, nothing for the instrument to crow over. The sums he added were, though large, small enough for him to check by simple arithmetic. The instrument told, it seemed, no lies and might be trusted with huge multiplications and even square roots. Then there was a knocking at his door. It was April Elgar in plastic rainhood and raincoat. It was hard to tell whether her face had been irrigated by rain or was being irrigated by tears. She said:

'I've moved in here. I can't stand the bastards.'

'You mean,' Enderby asked, 'in *here*?'

'Not in here, stoopid. In the hotel. Just down the corridor.' And then she sat on the nearer bed, that on which Enderby, in shirt, trousers and socks, had been lying calculating, and wept. Enderby sat next to her. He said:

'Take those things off. The outer ones, I mean. Then tell me why. Crying, that is. Not that there's any reason why you should. Explain, I mean. We all ought to be crying all the bloody time.' She needed, Enderby could see, comfort, so he put his arms about her. So, in his arms and in plastic rainwear, she sobbed. He patted the plastic rainwear, going 'There, there.' And then: 'Insulted you, did they, those white bastards? And then there's coming away from home and leaving your mother and your kids, a known loving ambience, and meeting sneering swine making uncalled-for references to your private life I took them to be, believe me, I don't believe any of it, I know you, it's the snarl the jealous world delivers to talent and beauty, there, there.' He nearly added, unthinking, his stepmother's cantrip: *Cry more and you'll pee less.* She stopped crying very suddenly, wiped her eyes and face vigorously on Enderby's shirt, then said, as all women were supposed to say, according to Enderby's reading, in such circumstances:

'I must look terrible.'

'Not at all. Young, defenceless, and, of course, very beautiful. Now take that stupid rain thing off. Have you eaten anything?'

'Yeah, I ate dinner, and those bastards were in the dining room kind of jeering, and then I went back up and was taking a shower, and I said the hell with it, I'm going to where *my friend* is, so I got my bags taken down and I put on my raincoat and. If I take it off,' she suddenly began to giggle, 'you'll see the real me, kid. Divine fundament and all.'

'You mean,' Enderby gulped, 'straight out of the bath, shower I mean, ridiculous unclean American custom, and and.' His body stiffened except for one member, which couched morbidly flaccid. 'I see.' He added, obscurely: 'The casting of the die.' He superadded: 'You mean you *would*?'

'You talked about loving me till you die, kid.'

'It's not the same,' Enderby said, much perturbed. 'Perhaps I've been too dualistic, too Platonic. I mean, there are too many difficulties involved. Aesthetic, for instance. Beauty and the beast. Not that I'm ungrateful. But love, love, that's something different from taking that thing off. Please understand.'

'I see.' Standing, she put her hands in the raincoat pockets. 'I got in one of my bags in the room down along there what they called publicity pictures. Tits and ass and teeth and legs in gunmetal stockings and frothy lingerie. The kind of thing pimply kids fire their wad at. You know what I mean?'

'Yes,' Enderby said unhappily. 'Pulling their wires, or monkeys. Bashing the bishop. Alas, yes.'

'That the me you want, brother?'

'If,' Enderby said hangdog and noticing a hole in his sock where an uncut craggy nail protruded, 'I were worthy. Young, black perhaps or browner than I am. All I can do is love humbly and cherish dreams.'

'Yah, wet ones.'

'It's been a long time. I am what I am. But I mean what I say about love.'

'Yeah, and you don't have to prove it. I'm not God, Baptist or Catholic. But, brother, I forbid the worship of images. Think about it. I got to go and unpack. We got an early call tomorrow. First band rehearsal.'

'I'll see you,' Enderby said with relief, 'at breakfast.'

'Yeah, early morning nourishment. Wadfiring must take a lot out of you.' Then she left.

IO

'The signification in British, that is to say traditional, English is altogether – '

'There will have to be an emergency meeting of the – '

'Too late now. We open tomorrow.'

And so there had been a howling and scratching limping progression towards the moment of the first dress rehearsal, Enderby sometimes peering in at the screaming and shouting from one of the top doors of the auditorium, but Toplady always seeming to know he was doing this and turning to yell 'Out!' So Enderby had stood a short while outside, Lazarus at the feast of punching and hairtearing, listening to music which, whatever it was, was not Elizabethan. Instrumentalists who did not seem to care much for music except as a union-protected livelihood had been scraped in from all over flat Indiana, and these had demanded coffeebreaks at the very instant when, after several hours of paid unscraping and unblowing, they were bidden play. There had been disdainful dim men around copying band parts, but only after bitter sessions of negotiation with the head of the local part-copying union, who himself copied no parts.

'*Arse* is one thing, *ass* quite another.'

'That first word is a British perversion of that second one.'

'Ah, bloody nonsense.'

Enderby had been both surprised and fearful that he had no longer, save for one small thing, been called in to make emendations or compose new verses. Everybody had appeared resigned to the way things were, not knowing how to make them better, or worse, and sensibly doubting that Enderby knew either. So the second act had the Essex rebellion, the Dark Lady shoved into a dark jail, the Bard collapsing with various kinds of distress as the Ghost in *Hamlet*, which and whom (Hamlet) he kept, in bereaved father's guilt, calling *Hamnet* and Hamnet, his going home to Stratford to be nagged to death by Anne, but not before conjuring the Dark Lady as Cleopatra and seeing, about his deathbed, visions of her wagging her divine farthingaled ass to that early mocking ditty about love.

'New England puritanism would not admit the real word. Bugger it, man, look at Chaucer – *ers*. *Ass* is a euphemism.'

'The title will have to be changed. There will have to be an emergency – '

So that was it and there it was. Pay me and let me get the hell out. But Ms Grace Hope, who had previously disgrudged odd thin sheaves of greenbacks, had buggered off back to the Coast, first having quarrelled violently, in public too, with her husband the fag Oldfellow, who had been carrying on overblatantly with his understudy Dick Corcoran, the Earl of Essex. Enderby had brought his overdue hotel bill to the concourse of wildly but silently clacking typewriters to have something done about it and been sent, by circuitous stairways, to a little Viennese Kantian sequestered in a cellar, a refugee from Hitler's *Anschluss*, who would discourse charmingly on the metaphysics of money but would pay not one red cent out. Enderby had been, was, fed up.

'Believe you me, you will make yourselves bloody laughing-stocks. The title comes from – '

'Not even William Shakespeare is immune from censure. We have here a quorum, I think – '

'Some of them drunk.'

'That is uncalled for – '

He had assuaged his misery and boredom by raging around the small office, uncleaned, unvisited, that had long before been allotted to him, switching on the typewriter and mostly ignoring its invitatory hum, thus vindictively wasting the Peter Brook Theater's electricity, but also occasionally adding a pecked line to a formless poem he was allowing to accumulate, its theme Caesar (he, Enderby, unlaureled) and Cleopatra (she who these days uttered mostly a distracted *Hi* at him. Her dresser had arrived from New York, an Iras or Charmian of gross mammyish aspect who slept in the room next to Enderby's and laughed in her sleep).

> Nor will this quadrate marble crush
> Juice from the olive stone,
> No slave philosopher enmesh
> In marriage stone and moon.
> By narrow moongate let me in,
> Eased by the olive's gush.

He had had his chance, he could not deny it, but he had not wanted the chance, had he? Shakespeare would have understood, she not, never, either Dark Lady. Musing thus, he received a cold note ordering him to perform what seemed to be a final scriptorial office, namely to compose a kind of national anthem for Elizabethan England. He rattled off:

The babe's first breath
Is: Elizabeth.
The soldier's death
Is for Elizabeth.
Hail Gloriana, keep England our home
Safe from her enemies: Scotland and Ireland and France and Spain
    and Muscovy and the Holy Roman Empire and, it goes totally
    without saying, Rome.

Delivering it in an envelope (let them bloody well process that into something singable, the bastards) to the secretarial concourse, he had seen for the first time the presswet posters. ACTOR ON HIS ASS. Clever in a way. It could not be, though it was now being, considered obscene, since it was a citation from *Hamlet*, but its implication was totally vulgar. On a notice board he had read that the final dress rehearsal would be in the nature of a free performance for the schoolkids of Indianapolis and environs, three in the afternoon of 6 January, Twelfth Night if anyone was interested, and that in the evening there would be an obligatory party at the mansion of Mrs Schoenbaum. That party was in progress now. Enderby was having it out about the title with one of the board of governors of the theater trust, a hardware magnate named, it seemed, Humrig, retired and now, apparently, a fulltime churchwarden. He

123

drank teetotal punch, which few others there did. Enderby said:

'Anyway, it's not my responsibility – either the title or your own wretched squeamishness. *Ass* is *asinus*, a donkey.'

'You wrote the ah play.'

'I wrote something. Whether that something is still there I can't say. I did not go to the dress rehearsal, though I heard lots of ill-behaved schoolchildren. They seemed to enjoy it. On their level.'

Enderby turned his back on Mr Humrig and went to the improvised bar, which the mad son Philip and the grey black retainer were running together. 'Gin,' Enderby ordered. The mad son Philip whispered:

'I got this stuff spiked.'

'I beg your pardon?'

'Smell it.' A jug of murky orange liquid was raised to Enderby's nose and he got a whiff of surgical spirit.

'That,' Enderby said, 'could be dangerous.'

'Shit to them. That guy there plays piano like shit.'

He meant the haired *répétiteur* Coppola, who was crashing out what sounded like an atonal cancan, to which Toplady's ginger mistress and another girl pranced with raised skirts. 'Gin,' Enderby insisted. He observed April Elgar in a blazing scarlet directoire, from the look of it, nightdress talking earnestly to the black lad of the company, Sir Walter Raleigh for all Enderby knew, who counted points off on his fingers. Toplady sat glumly with talking elders on or in the deep couch. Enderby heard something about renewal of contract, probably nonrenewal. Toplady was perhaps for the chop for some reason, probably unconnected primarily with the ass business. Mrs Allegramente came up to Enderby and said:

'Leave the Irish alone.'

'Only too glad,' Enderby said, 'to leave the murderous bastards alone. It's not my concern anyway. If you're so concerned get over to Belfast and have your kneecaps converted to Quaker Oats.'

Mrs Schoenbaum did not seem happy about her party. She stood at an end of the room with the lawyer Elvin or Alvin or something, clad in black silk pyjamas with a gold caftan over, her hair, as previously, glued to a snapshot wuthering.

She seemed ready for a cardiac arrest when two genuine Elizabethans entered, late and tanked up elsewhere – William Shakespeare and the Earl of Essex, both bearded, wigged, ruffed, jerkined, slashtrunked, hosed. Enderby too had a profound tremor until William Shakespeare spoke in the accent of Cedar Rapids, Iowa. He cried:

'Greetings to ye all, let the nutbrown ale floweth, or, marry and egad, the iciclebythewalled martini.' He noticed Enderby and added: 'And all that sort of heynonnino shit.' Enderby growled:

'Learn your Elizabethan grammar before you start mocking it. The accusative of *ye* is *you*. And a profound heynonnino to you, fleerer and bad actor.'

'Do not,' said Humrig the churchwarden, 'use language of that sort in the presence of Mrs Schoenbaum.'

'Shit,' said the mad son Philip. 'Shit shit shit.'

'Philip,' his mother said, *'please.'*

'I wanna play the piano,' Philip said, 'and that guy there hogs it.'

'Welcome,' haired Coppola said, banging three Scriabinesque cacophonies and getting up with a low bow and an arm stretched in proffer. Philip drooled his way over and began to play something manic and unrecognizable. He cried:

'Dance! Dance!' Some obeyed. Enderby asked the grey black for more gin. Oldfellow Shakespeare was on to him now, saying:

'And what the fuck do you know about acting?'

'Enough to know that you're as much like Shakespeare as my arse or ass. And,' he added, 'your breath smells horrible.' It did too. Perhaps that was the origin of sodomy: avoiding partner's halitosis. Enderby got away and over to a corner where Mrs Schoenbaum's daughter was leasing her bedroom for half an hour for five dollars. Toplady and the conferrers got up with difficulty from the deep boat of a couch. Toplady cried:

'Stop that row for a minute.'

'Okay.' Oldfellow had followed Enderby. 'You try it, buster, that's all, you just try it.'

'I speak English anyway,' Enderby said, 'and I know the lines.'

The hands of Philip had been forcibly removed from the

piano keys. Toplady cried: 'A few words, friends. You've worked hard. We've all worked hard. Some not so hard as others, but let that pass. Tomorrow we open. Or rather tomorrow *you* open. My contract as Artistic Director of the Peter Brook Theater was due to end in March. By mutual agreement it ends as of now. Certain elements do not like the way I have been doing things. There's a feeling that I should have concentrated on ordure like *Abie's Irish Rose* or *A Tree Grows in Brooklyn*. I have not made the Peter Brook Theater a centre of entertainment. It is wrong apparently to take the drama seriously. Until my successor has been chosen things will be in the incapable hands of my sleeping assistant director Jed Tilbury. Bless some of you and fuck others. I go.' He went. Some watched him go, others turned to look at this Jed Tilbury, who was the black lad enumerating points, though now no longer, to April Elgar. He cried:

'Hey, man – '

'De party over, I guess,' said the grey black retainer. 'An a gud ting too,' in the manner of Mr Woodhouse.

'More gin,' Enderby said. 'And then call me a taxi.'

'You call you own taxi, man. I don't call no taxis for no one no how.'

Toplady's mistress was meanwhile looking for her left shoe and calling: 'Gus, Gus, wait for me, Gus.' The shoe found, she stopped on her way out to fix hatefilled eyes on Enderby. 'It's you,' she said. 'You brought bad luck, you bastard.'

'Not me, kid or baby or whatever it is,' Enderby said heavily. 'Somebody bigger than me. Leave well alone is what I say. And don't call me bastard.'

'Bastard,' she said and was off, crying 'Gus.' Enderby said to the grey black:

'You're a servant. Call me a taxi. But first more gin.'

'You not call me servant, man. I ain't no servant.'

Mrs Allegramente was now there, saying: 'Is he giving trouble, Edwin? Is he being racist?'

'You keep out of this,' Enderby said. And then: 'Ah, please yourself. Protestant Ulster for ever. God bless King Henry the Eighth.' Before going to the hallway to call himself a taxi, he went over to April Elgar and the black now revealed as Jed

126

Tilbury. To him he said: 'Congratulations are probably in order.' To her: 'I'm going back to the hotel. Will you come?'

'Why?' she said with a new pertness.

'Because the party seems to be over and it was a terrible party anyhow and we stay at the same hotel and I'm calling a – '

'Jed'll take me home,' she said.

From the tail of his right eye Enderby saw Dick Corcoran as Earl of Essex swill thirstily from an orange juice jug. Very sensible, do him good, all those vitamins. 'Right,' Enderby said. And then: 'A queer sort of time we've had when you come to think about it. Meddling with Shakespeare. All right on the night, though. As they say.' He saw now, coming in too late, Bodiman, Pip Wesel and Silversmith, all drunk and leering. The grey black retainer or hired man or whatever he was supposed to be called let out a great wail of distress. 'If,' Enderby said, 'those three start insulting you, let me know.'

'Certainly,' she said. 'I'll call your room and you can come back and hit them or something.' She spoke, for some reason, rather like the actress Bette Davis. Enderby knew now that it was far too late to start trying to learn about women. He sighed and said:

'That girl who left just then, the one who plays Queen Elizabeth I gather, says it's all my fault, whatever she means by *all*. Ah well, I suppose I must go and say good night to our hostess.'

'Don't be like that,' Jed Tilbury said. 'Nothing to be depressed about, man. Ain't the end of the world.' He showed many teeth, all his own, and added: 'Just what it's not.' It was only when a taxi arrived that Enderby realized what he might mean. Ah just died, baby. Well, let them get on with it. The taxi driver was prepared for a long literary conversation with Enderby. He was a young Canadian, down here visiting for the Christmas vacation, then back to Yorke University outside Toronto to resume work on his thesis, to be entitled 'Future in the Past'. About science fiction.

'Been reading some of it,' Enderby said tiredly.

'Only viable literary form we have,' said the Canadian. 'What did you say your name was?'

'Why are you driving a taxi?' Enderby said instead of replying.

'It's my brother-in-law's cab. He went bowling. Did I imagine it or were there two guys at that place dressed up like Shakespeare?'

'You didn't imagine it.'

'And what did you say your name was?'

'Enderby,' Enderby said. 'The poet,' with small hope of being known as such, not that it mattered.

'Right. I thought that was the name. And then when I saw these two guys it kind of rang a bell. Read that thing of yours if you're the guy that wrote it. It was in the *Koksoak*, hell of a name. About Shakespeare. What you ought to write is sort of SF Shakespeare, know what I mean? About some Martian landing in Elizabethan England and meeting Shakespeare and putting The Power on him. See what I mean?'

'It's the name of a Canadian lake, I think. *Not* pronounced Cock Soak. Yes yes, I see what you mean. Here we are, I think.'

'Yeah.' Meaning the Holiday Inn in Terrebasse. 'It's an idea anyhow. Although there's this theory that it's us are the Martians. We landed on this planet in prehistoric times and killed off the earthmen. We knew that Mars was dying, see, and saw the fertility of the earth through powerful instruments. Then the earth's lack of oxygen stunted our brains and we had to start all over again. Four dollars fifty.'

Enderby had a nightmare and woke from it, impertinently engorged, at something after four. He dreamed that he was forced to act the role of Shakespeare in *Actor on His Ass* because both leading man and understudy had walked out and there was nobody else who knew the lines. No question of cancelling the performance, too much investment involved, backers insisted that show go on. Enderby as Shakespeare went on stage and opened mouth but no words came out. The audience jeered and somebody threw a missile like a miniature moon. It hit his head and cracked open and covered him with olive oil. The audience roared. Enderby awoke sweating. Thank God it was only a dream, nightmare rather.

II

'I mean, damn it, look at me,' Enderby cried supererogatorily, for that was precisely what they were doing. The cast, with two notable exceptions and a nailbiting Jed Tilbury in charge, his colour today like that of a very old elephant, sat around in the greenroom, looking at Enderby. The coffee machine needed repair, and it growled within like a stomach and infrequently, into a plastic yellow bucket, gushed slop. 'Why can't somebody else do it, for Christ's sake?'

'Tomorrow night, okay,' Jed Tilbury said. 'Floyd learning the lines and Shep learning the other lines.' He meant a long youth in a lumberjack outfit with a yellow coxcomb and another, older, in jeans and a Monto Carlo Grand Prix tee-shirt. 'But there's tonight, man, and it's the opening and you got this British voice and you wrote the goddamned thing. And you'll have a wig and a beard – and, Jesus, you got Ape here to push you through it, and Oldfellow's songs are taped, and, Jesus, you got to do it, man.' Enderby looked at the sweating youth, not so blackly cocky as he had been, a lot on the poor bastard's plate. 'And it's Ape's show, we know that, she push you through.'

'Yes,' Enderby said, with some bitterness. '*Ape.*' April Elgar sat there in a mauve track or jump suit looking rested, as though after some great black night of black amation, her own kind, right. Baby, ah just died. 'Goats and monkeys. Actor on his ass. Shakespeare reduced to the animalistic was bad enough. Now Shakespeare's reduced to me. Besides, I don't belong to the appropriate union.'

'Ah, fuck that,' somebody said.

'You're a poet,' April Elgar said without warmth. 'You got that in common.'

'I fear,' Enderby said, 'I fear – You lot are actors, and that means you're superstitious. That fag Oldfellow would have made Shakespeare just vulgar. I'd make him absurd. I can't do it.'

'Oh Jesus God.' Jed Tilbury's black emotional lability began to show. 'I got this job to do, can't you see that, man? I got to put this show on now Gus Toplady has slung. I got a career to think of, man.' He began to cry. As Enderby had half-expected, April Elgar did a there there patting act and even kissed his limp hand. Call of the blood, fellow melanoid in distress. Just died. One of the girls from the secretarial concourse came pertly in to announce:

'Pete Oldfellow's still blacked out with concussion. Dick Corcoran has this broken arm they've set and cuts and bruises. And he's charged with drunk driving and damaging public property. A mailbox it was. That was the Illinois police on the line.'

'Orange juice,' Enderby said. 'I should have warned him. I didn't think, blast it.'

'What in the hell did they think they were doing?' Jed Tilbury cried. 'Wearing those goddamn costumes too?'

'They might have been in drag,' somebody said. 'Fart in gales or whatever they're called.'

'And the car,' the girl said, 'is a writeoff. Lucky to be alive, the police say.'

'No sense,' Jed Tilbury said with sad weight, 'of professional responsibility.'

'And,' said the girl, 'we have to tell the press and the radio and the TV. About cancellation.'

'Yeah,' bowed Jed Tilbury said, 'we gonna cancel.'

'Lifelong love and devotion,' April Elgar said obscurely, though not, in a second or so, to Enderby. 'Let's see some of that. We don't cancel. Stick your ass on the line. You going to do it.'

'Oh God oh God,' Enderby moaned. 'What have I to lose? The ultimate tomfoolery.'

'You just pretend,' she said, 'that you're acting a Baptist

minister. The words are different, that's all.' Most frowned, not understanding.

Jed Tilbury showed both relief and the concern of immediate problems. 'We got to do a run through,' he said. 'Start now.'

'No rehearsals,' Enderby said. 'I know my own lines.'

'Yeah, but there been some changes – '

'About which I was not consulted. And I was barred from your bloody rehearsals. The joke, the man who wrote the bloody thing, that's all. Not one of you spoke up.'

'That's not true,' April Elgar said. 'It doesn't matter, but that's not true.'

'All right, thanks. So I get up on that stage as William Shakespeare, and you'd better all pray hard that the man himself doesn't punch through the bloody shoddy thing from the shades. Perhaps you'd better arrange a quick seance with Mrs Allegramente, if that's her real name, stupid bitch always going on about the sufferings of Northern Ireland, knows sod all about it. Get the enigmatic voice of the Bard on the hot line. Bugger everything and everybody.' He got stiffly up, the minor poet daring to be Shakespeare, Marsyas who was flayed for his temerity, and then hurried stiffly out to the nearest toilet. There he was urgently drained like a sump. Awaiting him outside was April Elgar. She said:

'You'll be all right. Just be yourself. If they laugh, okay they laugh. I don't think they going to laugh. You care for Shakespeare, that's got to come out.'

'That's the bloody trouble.' And then: 'What did you do last night?'

'No business of yours, sonny.'

'*Tell me.*'

'No, I don't tell you. You want to be jealous, okay you be jealous. Then you don't have to act jealous tonight. It's pretty hard to act jealous.' And then: 'You got no claim on me.'

'Love,' Enderby said heavily. 'Love, love. No, no claim, you're right. Love. I'm going off now to get drunk.'

'You better not.'

'*You've* no claim on *me*. I do what I want. What time do I have to report for duty?'

'You and me,' she said, 'are going to eat lunch, right. A couple martinis, okay. Then we go through the script. Then you have a little sleep. Then we come back here together. We give 'em all hell, you and me. Cabbages, sheep's heads, you got to despise them. Okay?'

Enderby sat in what had been, and might be again (emerging from blackout was the news), Pete Oldfellow's dressing room. He felt absolutely stone cold and indifferent as Pete Oldfellow's dresser, a retired minor actor new to the job, breathed Southern Comfort onto him. He sat and saw himself in a mirror framed with hot bulbs. Wig, beard secured with strong spirit gum. The Burbage portrait stared grimly back, though without earrings. Codpiece, hose, shirt, jerkin, ruff. Outside in the corridor there was scurrying and he could almost smell the sweat of nerves, as in a stable. A calm voice over a loudspeaker said: 'Fifteen minutes.' The dresser said: 'Your teeth okay? That bottom set looks kind of wobbly to me.' Enderby realized that he had left his tubes of toothglue back in his hotel bathroom. He gnashed at the mirror. They'd hold. The door opened and April Elgar came in in scarlet silk, *café au lait* bosom achingly on show. Her ink hair flashed with stage gems. She held out an envelope.

'Give 'em hell,' she said. 'My momma sent this. Enclosed, just for you. She sends her warm affection, happy in the Lord. We got a full house, baby. Don't open it now.' Enderby propped the letter against a Max Factor makeup outfit. 'There he goes.' They heard the faint voice of Jed Tilbury addressing the audience, apologizing for absence unavoidable of Pete Oldfellow and begging indulgence, part of William Shakespeare being taken at short notice by play's author the distinguished British. The audience's angry response did not come through. Soon, however, the farting of trombones and thuds of drums did. Overture and beginners. 'Luck,' she said and was off.

'You wanna a drop of this?' the dresser asked, bringing from a cupboard a fluted bottle of Southern Comfort. He was an undistinguished man on whom rested impertinently the distinguished though raddled mask of the late John Barrymore. Enderby could reply only with a headshake. He had no saliva and the mechanism of speech had totally to be remastered. He looked down with difficulty at sturdy legs in gooseturd hose. From these the power of locomotion had entirely departed. The feet just about worked still, however, and on these he slid towards the door. The door opened and Jed Tilbury, dressed presumably for Aaron the Moor, nodded at him. Enderby nodded back and said:

'Aaargh.'

Enderby was pushed by men in stagehand undress into total blackness. From his right an orchestra boomed and screeched to its final chord or what passed for one. Farther right there was meagre and dutiful applause. Enderby saw below the young bald Pip Wesel dimly lighted wagging a stick with a glowworm stuck to its end at dimly lighted music stands. There was a faint response to the stick and Enderby heard sung faintly from ubiquitous loudspeakers words he had himself composed:

> 'Bringing the maypole home
> Bringing the maypole home
> Bringing the maypole home
> Bringing the maypole home'

He now saw a woman in a kind of nightgown rocking a kind of cradle. That would be Anne Shakespeare, *née* Hathaway. He saw her more clearly as dimmers undimmed. He presumed he had to have a colloquy with her. To his surprise he found he could walk. He walked towards her. She was downstage in a pool of pink light. He spoke words:

'Aye, they're bringing the maypole home. You remember?' He saw there was a kind of casement standing on little wheels, unsupported by a wall. He went to this object to pretend to look out of it. 'A night spent in the woods, cider and cold meat and hot lechery. You overbore me as Venus overbore Adonis. I was cozened, caught, caged in a loveless marriage. I have a mind to go.' These words, so far as he could remember, were not in the script. It seemed to him that he was probably improvising them. 'Aye, a mind to leave you.' He blinked at the cradle-rocking Anne, who was not being played by the mistress of Toplady. There were coughs and rustles from the audience. Enderby spoke out more boldly. 'I have my destiny to fulfil, my star to follow.' He peered through nonexistent glass and saw nothing. 'More than my star – my constellation – she is bright this night. Cassiopeia is roaring lionlike in the heavens – an inverted W signifying my name. Will and Will in overplus. My name in the sky.'

From nowhere and everywhere the voice of the fag Oldfellow began to bleat:

> 'My name in the sky
> Burning for ever
> Fame fixed by fate
> Never to die
> At least I feast on that dream
> The gleam of gold, my fortunes mounting high'

At the third line Enderby realized that he was supposed to mouth those words, so he did. But it offended him that his voice should have become the voice of that now blacked out or just emerging from blackout fag. He strode quite sturdily downstage to the very edge of the apron and addressed the audience:

'A mask, a copy, a travesty. The poet turned into a motley to the view. You have heard of the *A-Effekt*? Alienation. I am not Shakespeare, he is not Shakespeare. We mock, we defy, we admit absurdities. You and you and you must all be punished.' He had heard those lines before somewhere. Yes, Eliot, *Murder in the*. 'Beware.' He strode back upstage. The song ended, to no applause. Male voices off began to sing.

> 'The Queen's Men
> The Queen's Men
> Not bread-and-beer-and-beans men
> But fine men
> Wine men
> Music-while-we-dine men'

'By God,' Enderby cried, 'the players are leaving. I will leave with them. They return to London, I spoke to Dick Tarleton in the inn but today. By God, if they will have me I will be one of them.' Anne ceased her cradlerocking and began to sing:

> 'Will o' the wisp, do not desire
> To follow fame, that foolish fire'

Enderby again confided in the audience: 'A lot of nonsense. This ginger-haired bednag, having nagged me to screaming, having scraped my loins dry, now tries the craft of quasi-melodic seduction. Listen to that voice. Would you be seduced by it?' And then, with great confidence, he strode off. There was applause which drowned the last lines of the song. He had, by God, got them.

In the wings he collapsed and was offered Southern Comfort and smelling salts, which they called smelling sauce. The thin girl who played Anne was on to him, ready to tear off his well-glued beard. 'You bastard,' she cried. 'You fucked up my song.' She was dragged away by ready shirtsleeved muscles. The wings were suddenly cluttered by mock-Elizabethans. Flats were wheeled in and off. Full stage lights screamed. The orchestra blared. And then there she was, divine farthingaled ass awag, down centre:

> 'The white man's knavery
> Sold me in slavery
> To an unsavoury'

Enderby was on his feet again looking down at a small boy dressed like a miniature Elizabethan adult. This boy proffered a sticky hand which Enderby vaguely shook. 'No,' the boy said in a profound if juvenile Midwestern accent, 'you gotta hold on to it.'

Of course, Hamnet his son. A property hand handed to Enderby a vague brown bundle. 'That's your grip,' he said.

Enderby and the lad toddled on and looked about them. London peopled mainly with prostitutes, some of them sitting sprawled, all bosom and legs anachronistically exposed, outside a door unupheld by a building. Enderby took the boy down-stage and addressed the audience: 'The title, incidentally, must not be misunderstood. *Ass* means a donkey. This child is meant to be Shakespeare's son Hamnet. His accent, you will notice, is unauthentic. Speak, child.'

The boy said: 'Is this London, dad?'

'Yes, my boy, this is a London apparently peopled by tibs, trulls and holy mutton. And do not call me dad. Dad is a term used only for an illegitimate father. In other words, only a bastard may use it. You, whatever you are, are not a bastard. Your mother and I were married in Trinity Church, Stratford. Ah, I wonder if that is Philip Henslowe.' Some members of the audience seemed to consider all this funny. Enderby went up to an actor who was frowning over a daybook and addressed him. 'You are Master Henslowe? In charge of the Rose Play-house on the Bankside? I have a play for you.'

'Ah, Jesus, will they never give up?'

It went rather well, Enderby thought, except that the small lad insisted on holding on to his hand while he was trying to gesture. He was forced to say: 'Go in there, Hamnet my boy, and play with the pretty ladies.' And he banged the boy's bottom thither. One way of getting him off. Unfortunately he collided with Ned Alleyn coming out, buttoning.

There was a kind of ballet with people carrying posters on sticks: TITUS ANDRONICUS; HENRY VI PART ONE; HENRY VI PART TWO – Finally there came RICHARD III. All Enderby had to do was to stand and watch and leave the work to others. But he had not to forget to note ostentatiously the passing of a message from April Elgar through her duenna to Dick Burbage. He was dragged off by a mass of exiters only to be pushed on later to find himself alone with the Dark Lady. He gulped. There was a frilled and tasselled daybed upstage. Downstage she sat combing her hair in an Elizabethan negligée. This was to be a love scene.

'Who are you, sir?'

'Madam, I noted at the play you did tender a message to Master Dick Burbage. You bade him come meet you here but be announced for discretion as Richard the Third. But, madam, I am the creator, with a little help from the historians, of that reprehensible humpback. I am William Shakespeare, madam.' Enderby glanced timidly up at the flies, whose lord might launch flyshit, at the enskied bard's request, to punish the Marsyas temerity of that identification. Then he said: 'Will you not like better a visit from a king maker than from a mere king?'

'What do you want of me, sir?'

'To see closer your beauty,' Enderby proclaimed, 'and to,' declaimed, 'admire it.' He heard a donnish querulousness in his tones and subdued it with a not too proper gruffness. 'It is a special and translunary loveliness not much seen, alack, in our pale and shivering clime that enthroned Sol disdains to visit. A sore lack, alack. But how do we define beauty? As that special property in woman, and in man too for such as are so given, that ah generates love. Seeing your beauty, I love it. And must I not love the possessor of that beauty? Ah, madam, I long to take you in mine arms. Love, aye, love, love. Love.'

That was her cue for song, but Pip Wesel the MD was slow to pick it up. Only when Enderby growled the word once more, frowning at the orchestra and, while his hand was in, the audience too, did the jazzy chords of exordium thump. She sang. Enderby blinked at her, still and watching. That lower denture, damn it, felt loose. He wondered whether he should go downstage and talk to the audience in good A-Effekt manner, explain that in point of biographical fact what they were now observing, except for the song, probably truly happened, but, in fact or true truth, she played on the virginals, so called because, and there was a sonnet about it, though Shakespeare got the meaning of the term jacks wrong. But then the song ended, and he beamed as she got her due meed of applause. No doubt about it, she swung both voice and d.v.a. to remarkable effect. He forgot his line, beaming. She fed it to him.

'Do I sing to your satisfaction, sirrah?'

He could see the spit of her sibilants in the spot beam. He shook his head and said: 'Not sirrah, no. That's by way of insult. Sir will do nicely. Aye, madam, you sing prettily. Can you dance as well?'

'I can dance the galliard and the high lavolta and eke the heels-in-the-air.'

'I thank you for that eke, more expressive than also, however much it may be taken for a mouse stirring.' By God, now it was coming. 'Can you dance the dance called the Beginning of the World?'

'Nay, sir, I know it not.'

'Then, madam, I will teach you.' And he, kicking out the Enderby as unworthy and becoming solely, though with a loose lower denture, Shakespeare, advanced upon her, upstage as she already was and near to that daybed. He clipped her in Shakespeare's arms and did buss her rouged lips. His or Shakespeare's heart beat hard and hot. Had having and in quest to have. All was justified; this was, by God, no more than aesthetic duty. He had her on that daybed and lay upon her. *For Christ's sake* her occluded mouth tried to utter. He mouthed juicily the

137

smooth brown of her wholly exposed shoulders and then, obeying Shakespeare's own Venus, Anne Hathaway really, strayed lower where the. *By God, madam, I have thee, I love, I love.* He was aware of the sturdy filling of his codpiece, really inside now, Mercutio, Benvolio, the codpieced lot of them. Then he heard a voice saying:

'Madam, Richard the Third is here.'

He tried to get his line out but could not. There were certain necessities that obliterated the obligations of art. Nay, more – was it not said that if a man made love on a railway line with an express train fast approaching he must say to himself that the driver had brakes and he not? Enderby was brakeless. But his panting succuba thrust him away and called:

'Tell him William the Conqueror came before – '

Then a whistle shrilled. That was the express coming. Bugger it, it had brakes, had it not? But it sounded like a police whistle. The watch had caught him at it, towsing in public, hale him before the Puritan magistrates for foul fornication. But the man who, to Enderby's surprise and Shakespeare's disgust, had just walked on the stage was in the costume of the twentieth century, that was to say a drab raincoat. He blew, as he had evidently blown before, his whistle, and then he addressed the audience. Enderby could not clearly hear what he said; he disdained the forward tone projection of the actor, though he said something about the actors' union. He pointed at Enderby, or Shakespeare, apparently to indicate that here was a foul fault and a sinful wight, to wit a non union member. Performance discontinued. Union regulation. Enderby, still clipping April Elgar, though looking towards the little expostulator with open mouth, now leapt off her and strode down, aware dimly of intercrucial wetness, to the edge of the apron and tried to push the man off. The man, who wore glasses that were filled with stage light, hit back. Enderby cried to the audience:

'I'm not acting now so this bastard here has no right to shove at me like that. Can you imagine such a monstrosity occurring at a stage performance in Shakespeare's own day? Shakespeare looks down from the heavens in disgust. Union rules, quotha. Devices of protection have become devices for dealing the death of the drama. Only one performance ever failed to reach its conclusion in Shakespeare's time, and that was in the Globe playhouse in 1613 when *Henry VIII* was being for the first time presented and the thatch caught fire.' From nowhere, though it might have been the flies, the word *fire* was, with a howl, repeated. The house lights came swiftly up. Enderby now saw, very rawly revealed, real seated people ready to unseat them-selves, a lot of them, uneasily looking for the source of the cry or the source of the referent of the cry. *Fire.* 'Stay where you are, damn it,' Enderby yelled, as people began to panic their way into the aisles. 'There's no fire, I just said fire, that's all.' *Fire* came again. There was already the beginning of a dang-erous pushing out, that woman there looked as if she expected to be trampled. 'Come back,' Enderby called, 'blast it. Back, you stupid buggers.' And, to the gawping orchestra, 'Play, damn it.' Shakespeare on the *Titanic*. They began to play, though not all the same thing. The audience, which had seen on films audiences tumbling out from fires, ready to trample, tumbled out none the less, ready to trample. Bloody Americans, no discipline, too prone to panic.

'My last number,' April Elgar called to Pip Wesel. She got a lumpish four bars in and began:

> 'Love, you say love.
> What you talking about
> Is filthy philandering,
> Goosing and gandering – '

Some of the audience turned, some even considered reoccupy-ing their seats. Most left. A man lay in an aisle, not dead. A woman whimpered, looking for probably a child or a handbag or something. Enderby said:

'A pity. It wasn't going too badly.'

'Yeah,' April Elgar said, 'not too badly. Ah, let's go.' The stage was filling with stagehands and members of cast. *No fucking fire*, someone said. Enderby saw the union man in hot colloquy with Jed Tilbury. He pushed the union man in the small of the back with his, or Shakespeare's, nief. The man counted things, probably rules, off on his fingers.

'Some of this?' the fag Oldfellow's dresser suggested, proffering the fluted bottle. Enderby nodded: some of that. April Elgar nodded too. 'I only got the one glass,' the dresser said. Enderby now saw that he was wearing, had been all the time, the computer wristwatch she had given him for Christmas. He said:

'Never noticed. Nobody noticed. God curse everybody. First man to wear a wristwatch was Blaise Pascal. After Shakespeare's time. Stupid bugger that I am. Uncyclical future. Time a straight line. *Domine non sum dignus. Domina* too, for that matter. Got to get away. The shame of it all. The bastards owe me money. Where are the bastards?'

'That,' she said, pointing. She was pointing at the letter she had herself delivered. 'Better open it. Felt to me like more than a letter.'

Enderby sliced the envelope open with what had recently been Shakespeare's right index finger. Dollar bills, each of a hundred. Five in all. He frowned, puzzled. He read the note. It was from Dr R. F. Grigson and addressed Enderby as Dear Brother. Distressed to see how service in the Lord's name had brought to a stage of nervous breakdown, not uncommon in the vocation of pastor. Perhaps a brief vocation (crossed out and vacation substituted) might help to restore to health and renewed vigour in the preaching of the Word. The congregation had been glad to help. The widow's mite even. No mighty sum but still. God's blessings and much sympathy and affection. Enderby showed her the letter. She had already seen the money. 'Now,' she said, 'you better go home. I said they were good people.'

'I wonder,' wondered Enderby, 'how much he minded. I wonder if he'll have an air crash waiting for me. Or skyjackers or whatever they're called.'

'Everything going to be all right. He liked people to act, right? He was an actor first, right? Here everything going to be all right because of the publicity. One thing won't get in the newspapers, though. A man having to pretend to be William Shakespeare before he can dance the Beginning of the World. You sure are one great big pain in the ass,' she said.

'I have this poem to write,' Enderby said, having tasted with little relish the sweet fire of Southern Comfort. What he needed was a mug of tea, my kind of, with seven bags. 'You gave me something to write about.'

'Yeah, that was all it was for. Giving you something to write about. Brother, I been used for a lot of things in my life, but never before to give a guy something to write about.'

'Well,' Enderby said stoutly, 'poetry has to go on. Nobody wants it, but we have to have it. There's something else I have to write first, though. A little story. *Leave Well Alone* or *Leave Will Alone*, some such title. About Shakespeare. If he'll allow it.'

'You wanna get that stuff off?' the dresser asked. Meaning the beard and the wig and the 5 and 9. Shakespeare looked at Enderby from the mirror and coldly nodded.

12 The Muse

The hands of Swenson ranged over the five manuals of the instrument console and, in cross rhythm, his feet danced on the pedals. He was a very old man, waxed over with the veneer of rejuvenation chemicals. Very wise, with a century of experience behind him, he yet looked much of an age with Paley, the twenty-five-year-old literary historian by his side. Paley grinned nervously when Swenson said:

'It won't be quite what you think. It can't be absolutely identical. You may get shocks when you least expect them. I remember taking Wheeler that time, you know. Poor devil, he thought it was going to be the fourteenth century he knew from his books. But it was a very different fourteenth century. Thatched cottages and churches and manors and so on, and lovely cathedrals. But there were polycephalic monsters running the feudal system, with tentacles too. Speaking the most exquisite Norman French, he said.'

'How long was he there?'

'He was sending signals through within three days. But he had to wait a year, poor devil, before we could get him out. He was in a dungeon, you know. They got suspicious of his Middle English or something. White-haired and gibbering when we got him aboard. His jailors had been a sort of tripodic ectoplasm.'

'That wasn't in System B303, though, was it?'

'Obviously not.' The old man came out in Swenson's snappishness. 'It was a couple of years ago. A couple of years ago System B303, or at least the K2 part of it, was enjoying the doubtful benefits of proto-Elizabethan rule. As it still is.'

'Sorry. Stupid of me.'

'Some of you young men,' Swenson said, going over to the bank of monitor screens, 'expect too much of Time. You expect historical Time to be as plastic as the other kinds. Because the microchronic and macrochronic flows can be played with, you consider you ought to be able to do the same thing with – '

'Sorry, sorry, *sorry*. I just wasn't thinking.' With so much else on his mind, was it surprising that he should be temporarily ungeared to the dull realities of clockwork time, solar time?

'That's the trouble with you young – Ah,' said Swenson with satisfaction, 'that was a beautiful changeover.' With the smoothness of the tongue gliding from one phonemic area to another, the temporal path had become a spatial one. The uncountable megamiles between Earth and System B303 had been no more to their ship than, say, a two-way transatlantic flipover. And now, in reach of this other Earth – so dizzyingly far away that it was the same as their own, though at an earlier stage of history – the substance vedmum had slid them, as from one dream to another, into a world where solid objects might exist that were so alien as to be familiar, fulfilling the bow-bent laws of the cosmos. Swenson, who had been brought up on the interchangeability of time and space, could yet never cease to marvel at the miracle of the almost yawning casualness with which the *nacheinander* turned into the *nebeneinander* (there was no doubt, the old German words caught it best). So far the monitor screens showed nothing, but tape began to whir out from the crystalline corignon machine in the dead centre of the control turret – coldly accurate information about the solar system they were now entering. Swenson read it off, nodding, a Nordic spruce of a man glimmering with chemical youth. Paley looked at him, leaning against the parferate bulkhead, envying the tallness, the knotty strength. But, he thought, Swenson could never disguise himself as an inhabitant of a less well-nourished era. He, Paley, small and dark as one of those far distant Silurians of the dawn of Britain, could creep into the proto-Elizabethan England they would soon be approaching and never be remarked as an alien.

'Amazing how insignificant the variants are,' Swenson said. 'How finite the cosmos is, how shamefully incapable of formal renewals – '

'Oh, come,' Paley smiled.

'When you consider what the old musicians could do with a mere twelve notes – '

'The human mind,' Paley said, 'is straight. Thought travels to infinity. The cosmos is curved.'

Swenson turned away from the billowing mounds of tape, saw that the five-manual console was flicking lights smoothly and happily, then went over to an instrument panel whose levers called for muscle, for the blacksmith rather than the organist. 'Starboard,' he said. '15.8. Now we play with gravities.' He pulled hard. The monitor screen showed band after band of turquoise light, moving steadily upwards. 'This, I think, should be – ' He twirled a couple of corrective dials on a shoulder-high panel about the levers. 'Now,' he said. 'Free fall.'

'So,' Paley said, 'we're being pulled by – '

'Exactly.' And then: 'I trust the situation has been presented to you in its perilous entirety. The dangers, you know, are considerable.'

'Scholarship,' Paley smiled patiently. 'My reputation.'

'Reputation,' Swenson snorted. Then, looking towards the monitors, he said: 'Ah. Something coming through.'

Mist, cloudswirl, a solid shape peeping intermittently out of vapour porridge. Paley came over to look. 'It's the Earth,' he said in wonder.

'It's *their* Earth.'

'The same as ours. America, Africa – '

'The configuration's slightly different, see, down there at the southern tip of – '

'Madagascar's a good deal smaller. And, see, no Falklands.'

'The cloud's come over again.' Paley looked and looked. It was unbelievable.

'Think,' Swenson said kindly, 'how many absolutely incomputable systems there have to be before you can see the pattern of creation starting all over again. This seems wonderful to you because you just can't conceive how many myriads upon myriads of other worlds are *not* like our own.'

'And the stars,' Paley said, a thought striking him. 'I mean, the stars they can actually see from there, from their London, say – are they the same stars as ours?'

144

Swenson shrugged at that. 'Roughly,' he said. 'There's a rough kinship. But,' he explained, 'we don't properly know yet. Yours is only the tenth or eleventh trip, remember. To be exact about it all, you're the first to go to B303 England. What is it, when all's said and done, but the past? Why go to the past when you can go to the future?' His nostrils widened with complacency. 'G91,' he said. 'I've done that trip a few times. It's pleasant to know one can look forward to another thirty years of life. I saw it there, quite clearly, a little plaque set up in Rostron Place: *To the memory of G. F. Swenson, 1963–2094.*'

'We have to check up on history,' Paley said, mumbling a little. His own quest seemed piddling: all this machinery, organization, expertise in the service of a rather mean inquiry. 'I have to know whether William Shakespeare really wrote those plays.'

Swenson, as Paley expected, snorted. 'A nice sort of thing to want to find out,' he said. 'He's been dead six hundred and fifty years, is it, and you want to prove that there's nothing to celebrate. Not,' he added, 'that that sort of thing is much in my line. I've never had much time for poetry. Aaaah.' He interposed his own head between Paley's and the screen, peering. The pages of the atlas had been turned; now Europe alone swam towards them. 'Now,' Swenson said, 'I must set the exactest course of all.' He worked at dials, frowning but humming happily, then beetled at Paley, saying: 'Oughtn't you to be getting ready?'

Paley blushed that, with so huge a swathe of the cosmos spent in near idleness, he should have to rush things as they approached their port. He took off his single boilersuit of a garment and drew from the locker his Elizabethan fancy dress. Shirt, trunks, codpiece, doublet, feathered French hat, slashed shoes – clothes of synthetic cloth that was an exact simulacrum of old-time weaving, the shoes of good leather handmade. And then there was the scrip with its false bottom: hidden therein was a tiny two-way signaller. Not that, if he got into difficulties, it would be of much use: Swenson was (and these were strict orders) to come back for him in a year's time. The signaller was to show where he was and that he was still there, a guest of the past, really a stowaway. Swenson had to move on yet farther into timespace: Professor Shimmins had to be picked

145

up in FH78, Dr Guan Moh Chan in G210, Paley collected on the way back. Paley tested the signaller, then checked the open and honest contents of his scrip: chief among these was a collection of the works of William Shakespeare. The plays had been copied from a facsimile of the First Folio in fairly accurate Elizabethan script; the paper too was an acid-free imitation of the coarse stuff Elizabethan dramatists had been said to use. For the rest, Paley had powdered prophylactics in little bags and, most important, gold – angels firenew, the odd portague, écus.

'Well,' Swenson said with the faintest tinge of excitement, 'England, here we come.' Paley looked down on familiar river shapes – Tees, Humber, Thames. He gulped, running through his drill swiftly. 'Countdown starts now,' Swenson said. A syntheglott in the port bulkhead began ticking off cold seconds from 300. 'I'd better say goodbye then,' Paley gulped, opening the trap in the deck which led to the tiny jetpowered very-much-one-man aircraft. 'You should come down in the Thames estuary,' Swenson said. '*Au revoir*, not goodbye. I hope you prove whatever it is you want to prove.' 200 – 199 – 198. Paley went down, settled himself in the seat, checked the simple controls. Waiting took, it seemed, an age. He smiled wryly, seeing himself, an Elizabethan, with his hands on the controls of a twenty-third century miniature jet aircraft. 60 – 59 – 58. He checked his Elizabethan vowels. He went over his fictitious provenance: a young man from Norwich with stage ambitions ('I have writ a play and a goodly one'). The syntheglott, booming here in the small cabin, counted to its limit. 4 – 3 – 2 – 1.

Zero. Paley zeroed out of the mothership, suddenly calm, then elated. It was moonlight, the green countryside slept. The river was a glory of silver. His course had been preset by Swenson; the control available to him was limited, but he came down smoothly on the water. What he had to do now was ease himself to the shore. The little engine purred as he steered in moonlight. The river was broad here, so that he seemed to be in a world all water and sky. The moon was odd, bigger than it should by rights have been, with straight markings like fabled Martian canals. The shore neared – it was all trees, sedge, thicket; there was no sign of habitation, not even of another craft. What would another craft have thought, sighting him?

He had no fears about that: with its wings folded, the little airboat looked, from a distance, like some nondescript barge, so well had it been camouflaged. And now, to be safe, he had to hide it, cover it with elmboughs and sedge greenery. But first, before disembarking, he must set the timeswitch that would, when he was safe ashore, render the metal of the fuselage high-charged, lethally repellent of all would-be boarders. It was a pity, but there it was. It would switch off automatically in a year's time, in twelve months to a day. Meanwhile, what myths, what madness would the curious examiner, the chance finder generate, tales uncredited by sophisticated London.

Launched on his night's walk upriver, Paley found the going easy enough. The moon lighted fieldpaths, stiles. Here and there a small farmhouse slept. Once he thought he heard a distant whistled tune. Once he thought he heard a distant town clock strike. He had no idea of the month or day or time of the night, but he guessed that it was late spring and some three hours or so off dawn. The year 1595 was certain, according to Swenson. Time functioned here as on true Earth, and two years before Swenson had taken a man to Muscovy, where they computed according to the Christian calendar, and the year had been 1593. That man had never come back, eaten by bears or something. Paley, walking, found the air gave good rich breathing, but from time to time he was made uneasy by the unfamiliar configurations of the heavens. There was Cassiopeia's Chair, Shakespeare's first name's drunken initial, but there were constellations he had not seen before. Could the stars, as the Elizabethans themselves believed, modify history? Could this Elizabethan London, because it looked up at stars unknown on true Earth, be identical with that other one which was known only from books? Well, he would soon know.

London did not burst upon him, a monster of grey stone and black and white wood. It came upon him gradually and gently, houses set in fields and amid trees, the cool suburbs of the wealthy. And then, a muffled trumpet under the sinking moon, the Tower and its sleeping ravens. Then came the crammed crooked houses, all at rest. Paley breathed in the smell of this late spring London, and he did not like what he smelled. It was a complex of old rags and fat and dirt, but it was also a smell he knew from a time when he had flipped over to Borneo

147

and timidly touched the periphery of the jungle: it was, somehow, a jungle smell. As if to corroborate this, a howl arose in the distance, but it was a dog's howl. Dogs, dogges, man's best friend, here in outer space; dog howling to dog across the inconceivable vastness of the cosmos. And then came a human voice and the sound of boots on cobbles. 'Four of the clock and a fine morning.' He instinctively flattened himself in an alleyway, crucified against the dampish wall. The time for his disclosure was not yet. He tasted the vowel sounds of the bellman's call – nearer to the English of Dublin than of his own London. 'Fowr vth cluck.' And then, knowing the hour at last and automatically feeling for a stopped wristwatch that was not there, he wondered what he should do till day started. Here were no hotels with clerks on allnight duty. He tugged at his dark beard (a three months' growth) and then decided that, as the sooner he started on his scholar's quest the better, he would walk to Shoreditch where the Theatre was. Outside the City's boundaries, where the play-hating City Council could not reach, it was at this time, so history said, a new and handsome structure. A scholar's zest, the itch to know, came over him and made him forget the cold morning wind that was rising. His knowledge of the London of his own day gave him little help in the orientation of the streets. He walked north – the Minories, Houndsditch, Bishopsgate – and, as he walked, he retched once or twice involuntarily at the stench from the kennel. There was a bigger, richer, filthier, obscener smell beyond this, and this he thought must come from Fleet Ditch. He dug into his scrip and produced a pinch of powder; this he placed on his tongue to quieten his stomach.

Not a mouse stirring as he walked, and there, under rolling cloud all besilvered, he saw it, the Theatre, with something like disappointment. It was mean wood rising above a wooden paling, its roof shaggily thatched. Things were always smaller and more ordinary than one expected. He wondered if it might be possible to enter. There seemed to be no protective night watchman. Before approaching the entrance (a door for an outside privy rather than a gate to the temple of the Muses) he took in the whole moonlit scene, the mean houses, the cobbles, the astonishing and unexpected greenery all about. And then he saw his first living creatures.

148

Not a mouse stirring, had he thought? But those creatures with long tails were surely rats, a trio of them nibbling at some dump of rubbish not far from the way into the Theatre. He went warily nearer, and the rats at once scampered off, each filament of whisker clear in the light. They were rats as he knew rats – though he had seen them only in cages in the laboratories of his university – with mean bright eyes and thick meaty tails. But then he saw what they had been eating.

Dragged out from the mound of trash was a human forearm. In some ways Paley was not unprepared for this. He had soaked in images of traitor heads stuck up on Temple Bar, bodies washed by three tides and left to rot on Thames shore, limbs hacked off at Tyburn and carelessly left for the scavenging. Kites, of course, kites. But now the kites would all be roosting. Clinically, his stomach calm from its medicine, he examined the raw gnawed thing. There was not much flesh off it yet: the feast had been interrupted at its very beginning. On the wrist, though, was a torn and pulpy patch which made Paley frown – something anatomically familiar but, surely, not referrable to a normal human arm. It occurred to him for just a second that this was rather like an eye-socket, the eye wrenched out but the soft bed left, still not completely ravaged. And then he smiled that away, though it was difficult to smile.

He turned his back on the poor human remnant and made straight for the entrance door. To his surprise it was not locked. It creaked as he opened it, a sort of harsh voice of welcome to this world of 1595 and its strange familiarity. There it was – tamped earth for the groundlings to tamp down yet further; the side boxes; the jutting apron; the study uncurtained; the tarrass; the tower with its flagstaff. He breathed deeply, reverently. This was the Theatre. And then –

'Arrr, catched y'at it!' Paley's heart seemed about to leap from his mouth like a badly fitting denture. He turned to meet his first Elizabethan. Thank God, he looked normal enough, though filthy. He was in clumsy boots, gooseturd-coloured hose, and a rancid jerkin. He tottered somewhat as though drunk, and, as he came closer to peer into Paley's face, Paley caught a frightful blast of ale breath. The man's eyes were glazed and he sniffed deeply and long at Paley as though trying to place him by scent. Intoxicated, unfocused, thought Paley

with contempt, and as for having the nerve to sniff . . . Paley
spoke up, watching his words with care:

'I am a gentleman from Norwich, but newly arrived. Stand
some way off, fellow. Know you not your betters when you see
them?'

'I know not thee, nor why tha should be here at dead night.'
But he stood away. Paley glowed with small triumph, the
triumph of one who has, say, spoken home-learnt Russian for
the first time in Moscow and has found himself perfectly understood. He said:

'Thee? *Thee*? I will not be thee-and-thou'd so, fellow. I would
speak with Master Burbage, though mayhap I am somewhat
early for't.'

'The young un or th'old?'

'Either. I have writ plays and fain would show them about.'

The watchman sniffed at Paley again. 'Genlmn you may be,
but you smell not like a Christian. Nor do you keep Christian
hours.'

'As I say, I am but newly arrived.'

'I see not your horse. Nor your traveller's cloak.'

'They are – I ha' left 'em at mine inn.'

The watchman muttered. 'And yet he saith he is but newly
arrived. Go to.' Then he chuckled and, at the same time,
delicately advanced his right hand towards Paley as though
about to bless him. 'I know what 'tis,' he said, chuckling. ' 'Tis
some naughtiness, th'hast trysted ringading with some wench,
nay, some wife rather, nor has she belled out the morn.' Paley
could make little of this. 'Come,' the man said, 'chill make for
'ee an th'hast the needful.' Paley looked blank. 'An tha wants
beddn,' the man said more loudly. Paley caught that, he caught
also the meaning of the open palm and wiggling fingers. Gold.
He felt in his scrip and produced an angel. The man's jaw
dropped as he took it. 'Sir,' he said, hat-touching.

'Truth to tell,' Paley said, 'I am shut out of mine inn, late
returning from a visit and not able to make mine host hear with
e'en the loudest knocking.'

'Arrr,' and the watchman put his finger by his nose, then
scratched his cheek with the angel, finally, before stowing it in
a little purse at his girdle, passing it a few times in front of his
chest. 'With me, sir, come.'

He waddled speedily out, Paley following him with pulse fast abeat. 'Where go we then?' he asked. He received no answer. The moon was almost down and there were the first intimations of early summer dawn. Paley shivered in the wind; he wished he had brought a cloak with him instead of the mere intention of buying one here. If it was really a bed he was to be taken to, he was glad. An hour or so's sleep in the warmth of blankets and never mind whether or not there would be fleas. On the streets nobody was astir, though Paley thought he heard a distant cats' concert – a painful courtship, just as on true Earth. Paley followed the watchman down a narrow lane off Bishopsgate, dark and stinking. The effects of the medicine had worn off; he felt his gorge rise as before. But the stink, his nose noticed, was subtly different from what it had been: it was, he thought in a kind of small madness, somehow swirling, redistributing its elements as though capable of autonomous action. He did not like this. Looking up at the paling stars he felt sure they too had done a sly job of refiguration, forming fresh patterns like a sand tray on top of a thumped piano.

'Here 'tis,' the watchman said, arriving at a door and knocking without further ado. 'Croshabels,' he winked. But the eyelid winked on nothing but glazed emptiness. He knocked again, and Paley said:

' 'Tis no matter. It is late, or early, to drag folk from their beds.' A young cock crowed near, brokenly, a prentice cock.

'Never one nor t'other. 'Tis in the way of a body's trade, aye.' Before he could knock again, the door opened. A cross and sleepy-looking woman appeared. She wore a filthy nightgown and, from its bosom, what seemed like an arum lily peered out. She thrust it back in irritably. She was an old Elizabethan woman, greyhaired, about thirty. She cried:

'Ah?'

'One for one. A genlman, he saith.' He took his angel from its nest and held it up. She raised a candle the better to see. The arum lily peeped out again. All smiles now, she curtseyed Paley in. Paley said:

' 'Tis but a matter of a bed, madam.' The other two laughed at that 'madam'. 'A long and wearisome journey from Norwich,' he added. She gave a deeper curtsey, more mocking than before, and said, in a sort of croak:

'A bed it shall be and no pallet nor the floor neither. For the gentleman from Norwich where the cows eat porridge.' The watchman grinned. He was blind, Paley was sure he was blind. On his right thumb something winked richly. The door closed on him, and Paley and the madam were together in the rancid hallway.

'Follow, follow,' she said, and she creaked first up the stairs. The shadows her candle cast were not deep; from the east grey was filling the world. On the wall of the stairwell were framed pictures. One was a crude woodcut showing a martyr hanging from a tree, a fire burning under him. Out of the smiling mouth words ballooned: AND YETTE I SAYE THAT MOGRADON GIUETH LYFE. Another picture showed a king with a crown, orb and sceptre and a third eye set in his forehead. 'What king is that?' asked Paley. She turned to look at him in some amazement. 'Ye know naught in Norwich,' she said. 'God rest ye and keep ye all.' Paley asked no further questions and kept his wonder to himself at another picture they passed: 'Q. Horat. Flaccus' it said, but the portrait was of a turbaned Arab.

The madam knocked loudly on a door at the top of the stairs. 'Bess, Bess,' she cried. 'Here's gold, lass. A cleanly and a pretty man withal.' She turned to smile with black teeth at Paley. 'Anon will she come. She must deck herself like unto a bride.' From the bosom of her nightgown the lily again poked out and Paley thought he saw a blinking eye enfolded in its head. He began to feel the tremors of a very special sort of fear, not a terror of the unknown so much as of the known. He had rendered his flying boat invulnerable; this world could not touch it. Supposing it was possible that this world was in some manner rendered invulnerable by a different process. A voice in his head seemed to say, with great clarity: 'Not with impunity may one disturb the.' And then the door opened and the girl called Bess appeared, smiling professionally. The madam said, smiling also:

'There then, as pretty a mutton slice as was e'er sauced o'er.' And she held out her hand for money. Confused, Paley dipped into his scrip and pulled out a dull-gleaming handful. He told one coin into her hand and she still waited. He told another, then another. 'We ha' wine,' she said. 'Wouldst?' Paley thanked her: no wine. The grey hair on her head grew erect. She mock-curtseyed off.

Paley followed Bess into the bedchamber, on his guard now. The ceiling bent like a pulse; 'Piggesnie,' Bess croaked, pulling her single garment down from her bosom. The breasts swung and the nipples ogled him. They were, as he had expected, eyes. He nodded in something like satisfaction. There was, of course, no question of going to bed now. 'Honeycake,' gurgled Bess, and the breast-eyes rolled, the long black lashes swept up and down coquettishly. Paley clutched his scrip tightlier to him. If this distortion – likely, as far as he could judge – were to grow progressively worse – if this scrambling of sense data were a regular barrier against intrusion, why was there not more information about it on Earth? Other time-travellers had ventured forth and come back unharmed and laden with sensible records. Wait, though: had they? How did one know? There was Swenson's mention of Wheeler, jailed in the Middle Ages by chunks of tripodic ectoplasm. 'White-haired and gibbering when we got him aboard.' Swenson's own words. How about Swenson's own vision of the future – a plaque showing his own birth and death dates? Perhaps the future did not object to intrusion from the past, since it was made of the same substance. But (Paley shook his head as though he were drunk, beating back sense into it) it was not a question of past and future, it was a matter of other worlds existing *now*. The now-past was completed, the now-future was completed. Perhaps that plaque in Rostron Place, Brighton, showing Swenson's death some thirty years off, perhaps that was an illusion, a device to engender satisfaction rather than fear but still to discourage interference with the pattern. 'My time is short,' Paley said suddenly, using urgent twenty-third-century phonemes, not Elizabethan ones. 'I will give you gold if you will take me to the house of Master Shakespeare.'

'Maister – ?'

'Shairkspeyr.'

Bess, her ears growing larger, stared at Paley with a growing montage of film battle scenes playing away on the wall behind her. 'Th'art not that kind. Women tha likes. That see I in tha face.'

'This is urgent. This is business. Quick. He lives, I think,

in Bishopsgate.' He could find out something before the episte-
mological enemies took over. And then what? Try to live. Keep
sane with signals in some quiet spot till a year was past. Signal
Swenson, receive his reassurances in reply; perhaps – who
knew? – hear from far time–space that he was to be taken home
before the scheduled date, instructions from Earth, arrange-
ments changed –

'Thou knowest,' Paley said, 'what man I mean. Master
Shakespeare the player at the Theatre.'

'Aye aye.' The voice was thickening fast. Paley said to
himself: It is up to me to take in what I wish to take in; this
girl has no eyes on her breasts, that mouth new-formed under
her chin is not really there. Thus checked, the hallucinations
wobbled and were pushed back temporarily. But their strength
was great. Bess pulled on a simple smock over her nakedness,
took a worn cloak from a closet. 'Gorled maintwise,' she said.
Paley pushed like mad; the words unscrambled. 'Give me
money now,' she said. He gave her a portague.

They tiptoed downstairs. Paley tried to look steadily at the
pictures in the stairwell, but there was no time to force them
into telling of the truth. The stairs caught him off his guard
and changed to a primitive escalator. He whipped them back
to trembling stairhood. Bess, he was sure, would melt into
some monster capable of turning his heart to stone if he let her.
Quick. He held the point-of-day in the sky by a great effort.
There were a few people in the street. He durst not look on
them. 'It is far?' he asked. Cocks crowed, many and near,
mature cocks.

'Not far.' But nothing could be far from anything in this
crammed and toppling London. Paley strained to keep his
sanity. Sweat dripped from his forehead and a drop caught on
the scrip which he hugged to himself like a stomachache. He
examined the drop as he walked, stumbling often on the
cobbles. A drop of salty water from his pores. Was it of this
alien world or of his own? If he cut off his hair and left it lying,
if he dunged in that foul jakes there from which a three-headed
woman now appeared, would this B303 London reject it, as a
human body will reject a grafted kidney? Was it perhaps not a
matter of natural law but of some God of the system, a God
against Whom, the devil on one's side, one could prevail? Was

it God's club rules he was pushing against, not some deeper inbuilt necessity? Anyway, he pushed, and Elizabethan London, in its silver dawn, steadied, rocked, steadied, held. But the strain was terrific.

'Here, sir.' She had brought him to a mean door which warned Paley that it was going to turn into water and flow down the cobbles did he not hold its form fast. 'Money,' she said. But Paley had given enough. He scowled and shook his head. She held out a fist which turned into a winking bearded man's face, threatening with chattering mouth. He raised his own hand, flat, to slap her. She ran off, whimpering, and he turned the raised hand to a fist that knocked. His knock was slow to be answered. He wondered how much longer he could maintain this desperate holding of the world in position. If he slept, what would happen? Would it all dissolve and leave him howling in cold space when he awoke?

'Aye, what is't, then?' It was a misshapen ugly man with a row of bright blinking eyes across his chest, a chest left bare by his buttonless shirt. It was not, it could not be, William Shakespeare. Paley said, wondering at his own ability to enunciate the sounds with such exact care:

'Oi ud see Maister Shairkespeyr.' He was surlily shown in, a shoulder-thrust indicating which door he must knock at. This, this, then, at last. It. Paley's heart martelled desperately against his breastbone. He knocked. The door was firm oak, threatening no liquefaction.

'Aye?' A light voice, a pleasant voice, no early morning displeasure in it. Paley gulped and opened the door and went in. Bewildered, he looked about him. A bedchamber, the clothes on the bed in disorder, a table with papers on it, a chair, morning light framed by the tight-shut casement. He went over to the papers; he read the top sheet ('. . . giue it to him lest he rayse al helle again with his fractuousness'), wondering if perhaps there was a room adjoining whence came that voice. Then he heard that voice again, behind him:

' 'Tis not seemly to read a gentleman's private papers lacking his permission.' Paley spun round to see, dancing in the air, a reproduction of the Droeshout portrait of Shakespeare, square in a frame, the lips moving but the eyes unanimated. Paley tried to call but could not. The talking woodcut advanced on

him – 'Rude, mannerless, or art thou some Privy Council spy?'
– and then the straight sides of the frame bulged and bulged,
the woodcut features dissolved, and a circle of black lines and
spaces tried to grow into a solid body. Paley could do nothing;
his paralysis would not even permit him to shut his eyes. The
solid body became an animal shape, indescribably gross and
ugly – some spiked sea-urchin, very large, nodding and smiling
with horrible intelligence. Paley forced it into becoming a more
nearly human shape. His heart sank in depression totally
untinged by fear to see standing before him a fictional character
called 'William Shakespeare', an actor acting the part. Why
could he not get in touch with the *Ding an sich*, the Kantian
noumenon? But that was the trouble – the thing-in-itself was
changed by the observer into whatsoever phenomenon the
categories of time and space and sense imposed. He took
courage and said:

'What plays have you writ to date?'

Shakespeare looked surprised. 'Who asks this?'

Paley said: 'What I say you will hardly believe. I come from
another world that knows and reveres the name of Shakespeare.
I come, for safety's sake, in disguise as a man from Norwich
who seeks his fortune in the theatre and has brought plays of
his own. I believe that there was, or is, an actor named William
Shakespeare. That Shakespeare wrote the plays that carry his
name – this is a thing I must prove.'

'So,' said Shakespeare, tending to melt into a blob of tallow
badly sculpted into the likeness of Shakespeare, 'you speak of
what I will hardly believe. For my part, I will believe anything.
You will be a sort of ghost from this other world you speak of.
By rights, you should have dissolved at cockcrow.'

'My time may be as short as a ghost's. What plays do you
claim to have written up to this moment?' Paley spoke the
English of his own day. Though the figure before him shifted
and softened, tugged towards other shapes, the eyes changed
little, shrewd and intelligent eyes, modern. Paley noticed now
a small fireplace, in which a meagre newlit fire struggled to
live. The hands of Shakespeare moved to their warming through
the easy process of elongation of the arms. The voice said:

'Claim? *Heliogabalus. A Word to Fright a Whoremaster. The*

Sad Reign of Harold First and Last. The Devil in Dulwich. Oh, many and many more.'

'Please.' Paley was distressed. Was this truth or teasing, truth or teasing of this man or of his own mind, a mind desperate to control the sense data and make them make sense? On the table there, the mass of papers. 'Show me,' he said. 'Show me somewhat,' he pleaded.

'Show me your credentials,' Shakespeare said, 'if we are to talk of showing. Nay,' and he advanced merrily towards Paley, 'I will see for myself.' The eyes were very bright now and shot with oddly sinister flecks. 'A pretty boy,' Shakespeare said. 'Not so pretty as some, as one, I would say, but apt for a brief tumble of a summer's morning before the day warms.'

'Nay,' Paley protested, 'nay,' backing and feeling the archaism to be strangely frivolous, 'touch me not.' The advancing figure became horribly ugly, the neck swelled, eyes glinted on the hairy backs of the approaching hands. The face grew an elephantine proboscis, wreathing, feeling; two or three suckers sprouted from its end and blindly waved towards Paley. Paley dropped his scrip the better to struggle. The words of this monster were thick, they turned into grunts and lallings. Pushed into the corner near the table, Paley saw a sheet of paper much blotted ('Never blotted a line,' did they say?):

> I haue bin struggling striuing seeking how I may compair
> This jailhouse prison? where I liue unto the earth world
> And that and for because

The scholar was still alive in Paley, the questing spirit clear while the body fought off those huge hands, each ten-fingered. The scholar cried:

'*Richard II*? You are writing *Richard II*?'

It seemed to him, literary history's Claude Bernard, that he should risk all to get that message through to Swenson, that *Richard II* was, in 1595, being written by William Shakespeare. He suddenly dipped to the floor, grabbed his scrip and began to tap through the lining at the key of the transmitter. Shakespeare seemed taken by surprise by this sudden cessation of resistance; he put out forks of hands that grasped nothing. Paley, blind

with sweat, panting hard, tapped: 'UNDOUBTED PROOF THAT.'
Then the door opened.

'I did hear noise.' It was the misshapen ugly man with eyes
across his bare chest, uglier now, his shape changing constantly
though abruptly, as though set upon by silent and invisible
hammers. 'He did come to attack tha?'

'Not for money, Tomkin. He hath gold enow of's own. See.'
The scrip, set down so hurriedly, had spilt out gold onto the
floor. Paley had not noticed; he should have transferred that
gold to his –

'Aye, gold.' The creature called Tomkin gazed on it greedily.
'The others that came so brought not gold.'

'Take the gold and him,' Shakespeare said carelessly. 'Do
what thou wilt with both.' Tomkin oozed towards Paley. Paley
screamed, attacking feebly with the hand that now held the
scrip. Tomkin's claw snatched it without trouble.

'There's more within,' he drooled.

'Did I not say thou wouldst do well in my service?' said
Shakespeare.

'And here is papers.' He looked towards the fire with a sheaf
of them. Then he went to the grate and offered them. The fire
read them hurriedly and converted them into itself. There was
a transitory blaze which played music for shawms.

'Not all the papers.' Shakespeare took the rest. 'Carry him
to the Queen's Marshal. The stranger within our gates. He
talks foolishly, like the Aleman that came before. Wildly, I
would say. Of other worlds, like a madman. The Marshal will
know what to do.'

'But,' screamed Paley, grabbed by strong shovels of hands,
'I am a gentleman. I am from Norwich. I am a playwright, like
yourself. See, you hold what I have written.'

'First a ghost, now from Norwich,' Shakespeare smiled. He
hovered in the air like his portrait again, a portrait holding
papers. 'Go to. Are there not other worlds, like unto our own,
that sorcery can make men leave to visit this? I have heard such
stories before. There was one came from High Germany – '

'It's true, true, I tell you.' Paley clung to that, clinging also
to the chamber door with his nails, the while Tomkin pulled
at him.

'You are the most intelligent man of these times! You can conceive of it!'

'And of poets yet unborn also? Drythen, or some such name, and Lord Tennisballs, and Infra Penny Infra Pound? You will be taken care of like that other.'

'But it's true, true!'

'Come your ways,' growled Tomkin. 'You are a Bedlam natural.' And he dragged Paley out, Paley collapsing, frothing, raving. Paley raved: 'You're not real, any of you. It's you who are the ghosts! *I'm* real, it's all a mistake, let me go, let me explain.'

' 'Tis strange he talks,' growled Tomkin. And he dragged him out.

'Shut the door,' said Shakespeare. Tomkin kicked it to. The screaming voice went, over thumping feet, down the passageway without. Soon it was quiet enough to sit and read.

These were, Shakespeare thought, good plays. A pity the rest was consumed in that fire that now, glutted, settled again to sleep. Too hot today for a fire anyway. Strange that the play he now read was about, so far as he could judge, a usurious Jew. This Norwich man had evidently read Marlowe and seen the dramatic possibilities of an evil Lopez kind of character. Shakespeare had toyed with the idea of a play like this himself. And here it was, ready done for him, though it required copying into his own hand that questions about its provenance be not asked. And there were a promising couple of histories here, both about King Henry IV. And here a comedy with its final pages missing in the fire, its title *Much Ado About Nothing*. Gifts, godsends! He smiled. He remembered that Aleman, Doctor Schleyer or some such name, who had come with a story like this madman (mad? Could madmen do work like this? 'The lunatic, the lover and the poet': a good line in that play about fairies Schleyer had brought. Poor Schleyer had died of the plague). Those plays Schleyer had brought had been good plays, but not, perhaps, quite so good as these.

Shakespeare furtively, though he was alone, crossed himself. When poets had talked of the Muse had they perhaps meant visitants like this, now screaming feebly in the street, and the German Schleyer and that one who swore, under torture, that he was from Virginia in America, and that in America they had universities as good as Oxford or Leyden or Wittenberg, nay better? Well, whoever they were, they were heartily welcome so long as they brought plays. That *Richard II* of Schleyer's was, perhaps, in need of the amendments he was now engaged upon, but the earlier work untouched, from *Henry VI* on, had been popular. He read the top sheet of this new batch, stroking his auburn beard finely silvered, a fine grey eye reading. He sighed and, before crumpling a sheet of his own work on the table, he reread it. Not good, it limped, there was too much magic in it. Ingenio the Duke of Parma said:

> Consider gentleman as in the sea
> All earthly life finds like and parallel
> So in far distant skies our lives be aped
> Each hath a twin each action hath a twin
> And twins have twins galore and infinite
> And een these stars be twinn'd

Too fantastic, it would not do. He threw it into the rubbish box which Tomkin would later empty. Humming a new song of the streets entitled 'Leave well alone', he took a clean sheet and began to copy in a fair hand:

The Merchant of Venice, A Comedy

Then on he went, not blotting a line.